G R JORDAN

# The Bothy

*A Highlands and Islands Detective Thriller*

*First published by Carpetless Publishing 2020*



*First edition*

*ISBN: 978-1-912153-72-5*

*This book was professionally typeset on Reedsy.*
*Find out more at reedsy.com*

*To June,*
*for all the encouragement over my writing years!*

# Contents

# Foreword

This story is set in the beautiful Black Isle which lies between the Cromarty and Moray Firths, located in the north of Scotland. Although set amongst known towns and villages, please note that all persons and specific places are fictional and not to be confused with actual buildings and structures that exist and which have been used as an inspirational canvas on which to tell a completely fictional story.

# Chapter 1

The day was cold, a real nip in the air, but for Georgie Haskins this was no deterrent. The Jack Russell beside her ran here and there nosing in some piece of undergrowth as they walked along the tree-lined stretch, down to the overgrown mass that protected the beach. A mixture of brambles and other green plants now made up a jungle to cover the treacherous path down to the sand. But it would be worth it once there. Solitude, quiet, peace. So different from London and the reason she moved here.

Georgie was in a good mood today having left her lover back in bed, letting him drift off to dreamland after his nightshift. Ten years her junior, she had been surprised when he agreed to come to the highlands of Scotland with her, especially as far north as Inverness. But he was in love, at least that was how she read it. And she loved it. To have a man chasing her as she crossed forty, after years of hard graft and quick but expedient relationships in the city, was a delight. She was done with all that digging for gold. The precious metal was following her now.

The bracken and bramble at the top of the small cliff threatened to stop her walk, thorny strands covering the thin path that would zigzag down the slope. But she had not come this far to be put off by mere nature. Stretching out a gloved hand, she pushed back the foliage and then nearly fell over her little dog as he passed between her feet, pushing on ahead. Still, she was okay. Continuing down the path, Georgie made slow progress but was undeterred.

It was only her second time here but she hoped it would become a routine. Once the path was negociated, the whole of a secluded beach was your own. There was even a rock feature that opened up to the height of a person and that led to a separate small inlet of the tide, somewhere to sit and dip your feet. She imagined in the summer she could bring her Romeo down here and they could soak up the sun, if it actually got warm enough, and then make love in the sand. Maybe that was a bit much, as it was not total seclusion. But she might bare a little more than normal and tease him.

Now that was unusual. A thin column of black smoke was rising from the building on the grass verge at the sand. It was a bothy apparently, a place once used to accommodate those who could not get back home as it was too far or who were simply working away from home. Georgie was not too sure of the detail,but it was basically a small house with very little inside except a single room and a spot for a fire.

A streak of annoyance ran through her. Who could be here to ruin her peace? Who was interrupting her little paradise? She had come all the way from London to experience this, where the hell had they come from? And there was that bloody dog running over to say hello to them as well.

It took Georgie another five minutes to clear the path. As she set her feet onto the grass verge, her dog was barking at her, jumping up and down, excited. Reaching down, she stroked the back of his head, telling him he was a "good boy" and generally hoping he would run off in another direction so that she would not have to meet whoever was inside the bothy. Her mind was drifting back to this morning, joining her lover in the shower and taking the remaining energy the nightshift had not stolen. Yes, that was something to dwell on at the beach.

But the dog was on another wavelength. Despite having had the animal for eight weeks, she still had not decided on a name for the creature and so he was simply "Dog". Another experiment, now she was clear of London, but one that was still in the balance. Looking after pets was not as glamorous as she had imagined. She swore as the animal ran off to the bothy again and disappeared out of sight. No doubt the stupid mutt had gone inside. She was going to have to talk to someone now.

Walking slowly towards the building, and trying to get her face into a friendlier scowl, Georgie wondered at the lack of noise. Normally when Dog barged in on people there was a commotion, or maybe a friendly greeting and a bit of jovial debate. But there was nothing except his bark. The sun disappeared behind a cloud as Georgie rounded the corner of the bothy and she felt a chill from the November air, nipping at her cheeks.

There was something wrong. She first saw a leg through the door, slim and slender and very naked. But it was snapped, or maybe twisted into a direction no leg should be. A thought struck her that maybe she should call out, maybe there was danger ahead. But then she would be making herself known. Carefully, she peered inside the crude wooden door as it lay half open.

Her eyes ran up the naked leg, seeing a pair of bare buttocks and then the flesh of a girl's torso. Hell, she could barely be twenty, if that. Her heart thundered in her body as she looked for the face of the girl but found none. No hair on the shoulders. Nothing on the shoulders. Involuntarily she threw up, emptying her stomach of her light breakfast before continuing, her stomach somersaulting as she shook.

Georgie told herself to run. But her feet remained, a morbid curiosity making her step forward, her foot landing in her sick before she turned her head to her right. A man was there, white plump flesh, and a generous belly looking like a hairy blancmange. On scanning his naked form she noticed he was missing genitalia. There was a copious amount of blood emanating from him and once again the body lacked a head.

Again she shook before vomiting. There was nothing inside her now and she continued to vomit as she watched Dog sniffing around something. There were two heads at the end of the animal's nose. She had to get out. Through eyes obscured with tears, Georgie fought her way to the sandy beach behind her and desperately searched for her mobile phone. God, no. There was no signal.

Quickly she ran back and forth along the beach looking for just one bar but there was none. Gathering what strength she still had, she raced back to the track, up the small cliff and ran through gorse and other spiked vegetation, scratching herself. Then her foot missed a section and she fell, one leg dropping far below the other. She reached out with a hand grasping a spiked branch, but held it desperately despite the pain.

Pulling herself back up, she fought her way to the top of the cliff before pulling out her mobile again, seeking the signal bars that would bring her help. There was one. Thank God, there was one. Standing upright, she dialled 999 and waited for the operator to answer.

"Which service do you require? Hello, which service do you require?"

There was a voice speaking, but Georgie could only see those bodies and the lack of…, parts. She didn't want to say the words.

"They're dead. God, they're dead. You hear me?"

The police operator taking the now transferred call, spent the first two minutes listening to someone retch. There were tears and spit, someone struggling. But then she came back hysterically.

"It's on fire. The bloody building is on fire. They'll burn!"

# Chapter 2

Macleod washed his face and then stared into the mirror before him. It had been a good night. Although the play had been a bit more arty than he would have liked, the company was splendid. They had dined at that small Greek restaurant on the corner before heading to the theatre and he had listened to her telling him about her day; how she had had a particularly difficult customer and how he had refused to believe he had been parked illegally for the previous two hours. Despite the seemingly mundane nature, she had a way of bringing the situation to life so that he had laughed hard for what seemed like most of the meal.

"She", was Jane Hislop, resident of Glasgow but former scourge of the Cornish Town illegal parkers and ready-to-ticket traffic warden extraordinaire. A recent arrival in the city, Macleod had Hope to blame for this new union in his life. His junior partner in the force had taken particular interest in him after the events on the Isle of Lewis, where Macleod's marital past and specifically the suicide of his wife had resurfaced to his detriment during an investigation.

On return from the traumatic case, Hope had decided it was important that her boss had a chance to talk things through. She had insisted on his coming out to curry houses and various other eateries in an attempt to make sure he was okay. Unfortunately, Macleod, whilst finding the forced conversation difficult, did find himself enjoying the view of his partner across less formal tables. With her casual and what Macleod reckoned to be "highly sexualised" clothing, he found himself constantly staring across tables at curves he really needed not to be attracted to. Having Hope around in the office was a nice distraction at times but these more intimate settings were taking feelings off in a taxi that was only heading for her flat.

And so Macleod had decided he needed to get back out, "in the game" as it was crudely called, and find himself someone more appropriate to share these rekindled urges with. "Urges" was such an ugly word, he mused, especially considering the woman now asleep in his spare room. This move he considered quite shocking as they had barely known each other a month, but Jane was so very keen to spend as much time with him as possible. They swapped churches on Sunday, his formal Presbyterian congregation in the morning and her more charismatic gathering in the evening.

Tying his gown around his waist, he made his way into the small kitchen and began to make some coffee in the new filter machine Hope had purchased him as a gift. A noise from behind made him turn and he saw Jane at the door in just a towel.

"The water's cold, is your heating working?" she asked.

"Blast it. They said they had fixed it last week. I'll need to get on to them."

"Its fine, Seoras. I'll just grab a quick wash."

"Why not just come through and have some coffee first and I'll try and get the water going."

"Okay, but I could do with a larger towel, I could only find this one and I think it's a hand towel."

Macleod looked over the table and noticed that the towel in question was barely getting past Jane's hips. "Why did you pick that one? I left you a big one out."

"No you didn't. You left me this one, you saucy sod. I know your game."

Macleod feigned some shock, but his mind struggled to recall which towel he had left out. "Sorry, I didn't mean to. I wasn't trying anything-"

"Shut up, Detective Inspector. You've got me in your custody and I'm banged to rights. Or do I need to read you your rights?"

Macleod watched in amazement as Jane dropped the towel and walked over to him in a state of full undress. He had been playing it cool, trying to take it slow to make sure she wasn't spooked and now this. Her hand reached out and took his neck, pulling it towards her for a deep kiss. Her brunette hair, long and swinging as one, touched his cheeks and he felt alive. Stepping back from him, Jane stood hands on hips and he gulped. Her slightly off-white teeth were now beaming and he cast his eyes on a body that looked so good. She was just past forty but Jane was every bit as wonderful as he had hoped. Only slightly overweight, he adored every curve and could feel the excitement rise that his wife had produced in him at will.

"So, are you going to arrest me or what?"

How, at a time like this, the logic of whether premarital sex was a good option or an insult to his creator came to mind baffled him. Maybe there was guilt in there about his wife. Maybe his faith was accurately kicking in to prevent any folly. But his eyes roamed, delighting in this vision before him.

And the doorbell rang.

"Tell me you're going to ignore that for me," said Jane.

"Of course," said Macleod, wondering who it was. The doorbell rang again, violently, over and over.

"At least your eyes haven't moved," said Jane, and she was right. *Stuff it,* thought Macleod, *I ain't missing this. However far this goes or whatever we do, I am not killing this moment.*

He reached forward, taking Jane in his arms, and embraced her with a hunger that had been building for a long time.

Now his mobile started vibrating on the table. And then his pager went off. And then he heard the door thudding like the hounds of hell were trying to get in.

"I guess this might be important," whispered Jane.

"I'm so sorry. Do you have a dressing gown?"

"Yes, yes I do. But it's... You'd better get that."

Macleod nodded and made his way to the front door of his flat. Looking through the keyhole, he saw Hope McGrath, dressed in her smart and practical office wear. *Damn,* Macleod swore to himself, *at this time of the morning, it is serious.*

Opening the door, he gave Hope an angry stare. "I know, I know," said his colleague, "I wouldn't be here if the shit hadn't hit the fan. You need to get packed and quick. The boss wants us up north to the Black Isle. Some DJ's missing; there are two burned-out bodies and a mass of suggestion going around. I have the car outside, sir."

Macleod watched Hope swan past him towards the kitchen. *Do come on in then.* Their relationship had grown to a point where he found her taking certain liberties and it was hard to rebuke her. Maybe it was the attraction he felt, but whatever it meant, Hope was a lot more familiar than anyone else from the force.

Entering his kitchen, he pointed to the coffee machine. "See

I am using it. And feel free to make yourself one. I need to dress."

"Sure," said Hope. "Good night, was it? She wears a good perfume anyway. I recognise it, one of the expensive ones. Guess it must have been a late one if it's still lingering. Still, I don't blame you, work's been a bit busy lately and I'm find..."

Hope stopped speaking as a woman walked into the kitchen dressed in a sheer dressing gown that stopped at the knee. Underneath it was a black T-shirt that was too long and ran past the hips nearly as long as the short dressing gown.

"Hi," said the woman, "I'm Jane."

"Jane." Hope recovered. "So good to meet you. Seoras has said so much about you. It's good to meet you. I'm Hope, Hope McGrath."

"I could tell. He has mentioned you once or twice. I guess you have some bad news if you're here at this hour."

Macleod appeared behind Jane and ushered her into the kitchen. "I'm sorry, Jane, so sorry. I have to go. Up north and I don't know how long. But I'll ring. Soon as I know."

"Is it something bad?"

"We're the murder squad, Jane. It's rarely good," said Hope.

"Here," said Macleod, handing Jane a set of keys. "Lock up after you and keep the set. And... is that your dressing gown?" He gulped. "And that's my T-shirt. So you wouldn't have been wear..."

"I'll give you a moment," said Hope. "Be in the car when you're ready, Seoras."

Macleod took Jane in his arms. "I'm so sorry. But this is what I am. And this thing tends to happen. And I don't know how long I'll be."

"Its okay, it really is, you have to work, so go get some bad people. But tell me if it's going to be long. I'll come up. If that's alright, I'll get to you."

"You know you don't need to do all this gown thing and towel dropping, you know I like you just for you."

"Of course. But maybe I like it. Sometimes you don't feel very attractive at my age."

"Now that is talk I won't allow," said Macleod and he kissed her. "I'll ring, soon as I can."

"I know you will."

Macleod drank in one last view of this new chapter of his life before walking out of his flat, back to the old life that he knew so well. Sliding into the car, he saw Hope's eyes and the grin on her face.

"Shut up and drive. It's all your fault." *But I'm not elaborating on that.*

# Chapter 3

"You crafty dog, you!"

"That's enough of that. Mere friends and nothing more, so enough from you, Detective." Macleod turned away to look out of the window, a smile on his face.

"Friends, in a dressing gown like that. She's got her claws in you." Hope grinned with a passion as Macleod turned back to face her. No one else on the force would get away with such a comment but after she had held his counsel about his wife's tragic death and his difficulties coping with it twenty years on, he saw her as more than a colleague.

"And now work takes me from her. More's the pity. So what have you disturbed my paradise for, Hope? It's got to be important, banging down the door this early, knowing I had been out."

"Got two dead on the Black Isle, just above Inverness."

"I know where it is."

"Well, apparently they were inside a small building, a bothy on a beach. The bodies were burnt, but prior to that they were decapitated. There's a witness who saw the scene then left to ring it in. By the time she got a signal, the building was on fire."

"So there might be quite a bit left for us if they saw it that early."

"I'm afraid not. It's local retainers in the fire service, and it's also some way off the beaten track. Apparently they did well to get to it and prevent it spreading to any of the vegetation. Forensics are there but there's been nothing yet."

Macleod nodded. "Okay, so we have a mystery, two bodies, and someone who knows their identity needs hiding."

"Well, one might be famous, at least in a local capacity. There's a DJ missing from the local radio station. Didn't turn up for his morning show at seven this morning. He's not been home to his house and no one has seen him since last night when he left a local pub after a meeting with the radio station manager. Might be a start."

"Do you have the early reports?"

"Yes, in the back there, the blue file. You can settle back and read, it's a bit of a trip. I was going to fly but, to be honest, seemed as quick in the car and a bit of a good drive. Thought you might need some recovery time too."

"Whoa, easy. I'm past my fifties but I'm not in a graveyard parlour yet."

"Tell you what, though, she's good for you. You're like a changed man since we came back from the Hebrides. Like a weight's come off you." Hope cast a smile his way and Macleod enjoyed its radiance.

He retrieved the file and opened it. As his eyes glanced over the pictures and the writing, his mind drifted back to the woman he had left behind. *That dressing gown. And she said she'd come, come up to me if it was prolonged. Something's happening.*

* * *

They managed only one very brief coffee stop on the way up. Macleod had wanted to go the whole way without stopping, but at his age the bladder was not always a friend. On reaching the Black Isle, they headed towards Cromarty at the far end of the Firth and took a detour on a back road before they reached the town, arriving at a small steading on the south side of the eastern tip. A police car blocked the road on one side and Macleod could see the press already gathered. As he stepped out of the car, he watched them descend towards him.

"What's the latest, Inspector?"

Macleod stopped in front of a man in a grey suit who had shoved a recording device in his face. The man's greying hair was swept across his head, showing faint cracks of flesh. His white shirt lay open at the collar and he was wrapped in a green parka. It was nippy, but Macleod had expected a bit more class. Still, it was the press, bloody vultures in the main.

"I have just arrived," stated Macleod in a flat tone. "When I have something, I'll brief you at the correct juncture. Until that time, investigations are continuing. Good day."

He walked away until he heard the man comment, "If I was investigating with her I'd take my time too. Look at the ass on that." Turning on his heel, Macleod strode up to the man, who instantly put his recorder in Macleod's face.

"Something else, Detective?"

"Yes, actually. And please do quote me on this. *That* has a name, her name is Detective McGrath and she's a bloody good one. And if all you can do is gawp at her ass, as you suggested your colleague should do, then you really need to get with the times. I doubt your readership will take kindly to that attitude. Or maybe your rag has that sort of reader. Either way, you talk like that again about my colleague and I'll be required to arrest you for sexual harassment. Understood?"

The man dropped his recorder. Holding his grim stare, Macleod made sure the man felt small before leaving. He caught Hope's face as he walked past the police initial cordon.

"Needed said."

"I can handle it," said Hope.

"I know, but it pisses me off. Still, he got one thing right."

"What's that?"

"Nice ass."

Hope punched him on the arm. "She's good for you, bringing you out of yourself. It's good, really good."

"Work, time to work," said Macleod, approaching a police sergeant.

"Good afternoon, sir, Detective Ross is in attendance down at the scene. He'll be able to bring you up to speed and hand over the investigation to you. But it's a fair walk down a tree-lined avenue and then down an overgrown path. We took the forensic people in on a boat, but you'll want to see where the first informant was."

"And good afternoon to you, Sergeant. Is it that way?" Macleod pointed down a line of trees.

"Yes, sir. Do you have boots? Would be advisable."

"McGrath, get the wellies."

Hope nodded. Macleod turned back to the sergeant. "Where's the informant now?"

"In shock, sir. They took her off to Raigmore, the local hospital, as she collapsed twice during questioning. I don't think it was anything more serious with her."

Hope arrived with the wellington boots and Macleod threw his shoes to the sergeant. "Throw those into our boot, will you kindly?" The man nodded and then held his hands out as

Hope dropped a pair of ankle boots into his arms.

"I think you'd have managed in those," said Macleod.

"I'm not walking muck everywhere. It looks pretty wet up ahead." The Sergeant nodded vigorously.

The walk along the tree-lined route took fifteen minutes and Macleod found himself splashing through puddles. Letting Hope take the lead, he walked behind, keeping to her track. His mind was already churning through possibilities about what he was to see and he did not trust himself to negotiate the occasional jutting branch and overturned stump on the ground.

On cresting the hill, Macleod caught sight of the sea and a line of bramble and other rough vegetation on what he presumed was a cliff edge. Three police officers stood guard at that edge and they pointed him towards a small path through the pointy plant life.

"Watch yourself, sir, it's pretty well overgrown."

"I'm no child, McGrath," said Macleod who promptly felt his foot slip, sending him into a nearby gorse bush. "Blast it. Give us a hand, Mum," he grudgingly requested. Hope pulled him clear and Macleod focused hard on her back as they descended. *It really is quite treacherous. If an informant came down here, or came up, it would take a bit of time and effort.*

As they cleared the gorse, Macleod saw a small building standing on the edge of a beach, the last verges of grass around it. He recognised the smell of a fire but one tinged with human flesh. It had that choking feel and set off a trigger in your mind that repulsed you to the core, sending your stomach into a spin. The outer edges of the building showed deep black markings from the fire and he wondered if there would be much inside.

Figures in white disposable overalls were working inside a

cordon, and Macleod looked for the senior. Being out of his territory, he was unsure of the appearance of the forensic team members but he knew the senior was a woman, name of Hazel Macintosh. As he surveyed the scene, a small rotund woman seemed to be guiding things through a combination of a harsh but hoarse voice and a forceful stare emanating from behind a pair of large black glasses.

Walking up to the blue cordon tape, Macleod raised his hand and called out to the woman. "Excuse me. Over here, please. Yes, you if you don't mind."

The woman shook her head and turned to a colleague, delivering more instructions before making her way over to Macleod. "Yes," she said indignantly as she approached him. "Make it quick, sunshine, there's a lot of work to do here. Now, what do you want?"

"A briefing."

"Another one. Hang about and I'll get MacArthur over to you when he's done with the sweep by the fire."

Macleod now took his turn to be indignant. "My name is Macleod, and this is my show. I'm going to that tent over there where hopefully someone from the local force will give me a briefing too. Kindly join us at your first opportunity. And I'd suggest that would be within the next ten minutes. I take it you're Mackintosh?"

The woman reared up on her short legs and pulled down the hood of the white overall she was wearing. "Yes, it's Mackintosh, and round here it's normal practice to announce who you are if no one's seen you before, Detective Inspector. You'll find Detective Ross in the white tent with a collection of some of the gorier parts of the interior of this building. But I'll be there directly. And you are?" asked the woman, reaching a hand out to Hope.

"Detective Hope McGrath, pleased to meet you."

"Likewise. Now give me a moment and I'll give you your briefing, Inspector." The woman turned on her heel, pulled up her hood and started to firmly rebuke another forensic officer who had caught her eye.

"Let us retire to the said tent and await Mother," said Macleod.

Hope giggled and he flashed a wink in her direction. Despite the sickly scene, Macleod knew he was in a good mood. *She said she would come up if it was prolonged. And I think this one might be.* His mind briefly roamed back to that dressing gown and the woman inside it. *Yes, it might be prolonged.*

The interior of the white tent held a small table with several plastic bags on it. A larger bag was also atop a long table and Macleod recognised it as one that would hold body parts. A man was labelling items and when he saw Macleod come in, the man raised his head looking for identification.

"Macleod, looking for Ross."

"Aye, sir. Just behind me. Detective Ross," the man called out, "it's the Detective Inspector from Glasgow."

*At least some people recognise the name.* Stepping forward Macleod met the oncoming hand of an averagely built man with one lazy eye that seemed to stare off at something else. The effect was disturbing, as was the man's apparent lack of dress sense, his green shirt and rather dark tie not quite matching the silvery grey jacket and trousers. The brown shoes did not help either.

"Fraser. It's good to see you, sir. What do you need?"

"Just a briefing, Ross, from the top in case I've missed anything."

"Aye sir. Well, this morning at six thirty, Georgie Haskins was walking her dog, coming down from the path I assume you had to take to get here. She saw smoke coming from the bothy, just through the chimney, and made her way inside to find two decapitated bodies- one male, middle-aged, one female, younger- and promptly ran. She made her way back up the small cliff as her mobile could not get a signal here. As she made the call, she saw the bothy go on fire. When our officers got here, the place was fully ablaze and it took some time to get a fire crew here and deal with the situation. Meanwhile our informant collapsed twice and is now in Raigmore hospital."

"Raigmore?" asked Hope.

"The main hospital in Inverness," clarified Ross. "Since that time, we have cordoned off and brought in forensics. There's also been a report made of a missing person from the local radio station, *Monster*, one of their top DJs, Andy *Howling* MacTavish. He was due on the morning show starting at seven, but he never came home last night or showed up for the programme."

"Okay, I'm not familiar with him."

"Brash, cocky, very loud-mouthed. A long-term stable of the station too. Had a reputation as a ladies' man, numerous rumours in the papers of affairs and that but nothing ever proved. Ah, here's Hazel Mackintosh, in charge of scenes of crime."

"It's okay," advised Hope, "they've already met."

Macleod shot Hope a look and then turned to the newly arrived Mackintosh. "Thank you for your promptness. What do we have?"

"Hazel Mackintosh coughed like a heavy smoker and then spoke with a rasp. "Not a damn lot, Macleod. The place was badly burnt so I doubt I'll get any traces of fingerprints or threads as the entire interior was gutted. Behind you in the black bag is one set of remains but with teeth. The other body we are just moving now. We should get confirmation of ID from the teeth if we have a starter for ten, but otherwise the only thing I can really confirm is that they were decapitated. Also something was in their mouths. I found a small amount of plastic, shrivelled from the fire, in each of their mouths. It may have covered paper, may have been a protective cover, but that's really speculation.

"That's it for the inside of the building other than a canister of petrol also inside the building and seriously fire damaged. The fire officer is saying petrol as the chief fuel for the fire and I agree. I'm thinking there was a third party, however, as we found a line of sweepings, like someone was brushing away footprints in the sand. They ran from the bothy down to the beach. There's some disturbed shingle too."

"Thank you," said Macleod. "So, decapitated heads, something in the mouth, fire started by petrol and an escape path back to the sea. Get on the man's body and check the dental records against the missing DJ, Mackintosh. Ross, hold here and continue to supervise, Hope will give you our mobile numbers.

"We need to check the local reports for any missing girls, organise that, Ross, up to a month missing, please. I'm guessing the body behind me is the DJ but we need more information. Time to walk back to the car, Hope, and make for Inverness. But Raigmore first, talk to our informant."

As Macleod and McGrath reached the top of the small cliff, he watched her turn and look out to sea.

"Good place. Romantic, away from prying eyes, shelter if it's a cold night. Not easy to get to either. I doubt there's that many come down here in November. If I was young and besotted, this place would turn my head. You could get on with a lot of things here. Be as naughty as you wanted. Perfect shagging patch."

There it was, that crudeness in Hope. Macleod looked at her as she admired the view, took in her full figure. She looked classy, dressed slightly provocatively, but he had developed a fondness for her. Maybe it was that crudeness that made him think he could improve her. *Damn, I can be so arrogant at times.*

"Yes, a good place to court, McGrath." *Much better word.* "But someone was watching. This was premeditated. Petrol can, decapitation. And something in the mouth. This isn't a simple tiff, a jealous guy or girl. Someone was making a point until they were disturbed. But who and why?"

# Chapter 4

Walking towards the hospital building, Macleod gawped at the large structure before him. He hated hospitals. It always seemed he was in them to see people die. If not that then they had suffered serious wounds. Generally he thought them places with no cheer. But then you were only here if you were ill.

On entering the building, he sent Hope off to find out where their witness was being stationed during her recovery and waited in the small shop.  He saw the papers on the shelf and realised the late editions were starting to carry the story. Having driven up from Glasgow, it was now late in the afternoon and Macleod still wanted to see the people at the radio station before he set up his operations base. He picked up a copy and perused it briefly while awaiting his colleague.

A man walked up beside him and, with a policeman's eye, Macleod clocked him as late thirties, maybe forties, and quite trim. The blond hair was neatly parted and Macleod noticed the shoes, black and patent, cleaned to such a shine that the lights above him could be seen perfectly in them.

The man leaned over. "Don't look now, but there's a right wee bit of stuff coming up the corridor."

Macleod did not want to dignify the comment by looking

around, but he was intrigued to see who this man gauged as a “wee bit of stuff”. Turning his head, he saw a familiar smile. He laughed to himself before turning back to the man and announcing to him that the woman also had a brain and looked amazing in a swimsuit. As he walked over to Hope he heard the man let go a swear and the words, “Lucky bastard.”

“Five floors up, sir. What are you laughing at?”

“Nothing, McGrath, nothing.” But Macleod continued to chortle. Clearly deciding any further probing was unwarranted, Hope led the way to the main lifts in the hospital. As they waited for the doors, the same man from the shop walked up beside Macleod. As they entered the lift, the man joined them taking up a position opposite Hope and clearly ready to have a good look.

“What floor?” asked Hope to the man.

“Wherever you're going.” There was a brief stare from Hope and then the word “Five” was volunteered. Hope pressed the button and then looked off into the corner of the lift. Macleod, however, clocked the man looking at Hope, assessing her. *Can't blame him for that.* As the doors opened the man let Hope exit the lift first and then had to wait for Macleod to move before exiting himself.

As he walked down the hospital corridor, Macleod became aware the man was still following. As they stopped at the beginning of the ward, to use the alcoholic gel on their hands, the man joined them before entering the ward before them. Macleod saw him stop at a uniformed officer briefly and then enter a room. On arriving at the same officer, Macleod showed his ID and then queried who the man was. “Miss Haskins' partner, sir.”

Macleod let Hope enter the room first and watched the man's

face from behind her. The man's eyes shifted this way and that as he sat beside his partner, Georgie Haskins. As his face was becoming redder, Georgie Haskins spoke.

"And who are you? I've given statements to your people already, what else is there to say? It was bad enough then without having to revisit it."

"Apologies," said Hope. "I'm DC McGrath and this is DI Macleod. We've come up from Glasgow to run the investigation into what you saw, and, to be honest, we would like to make sure everything is covered. We realise you've had a shock and we'll try to keep questions to a minimum. But we do need to go over it again."

"Sorry, I'm too tired, can't you come back tomorrow? Neil, make them come back tomorrow."

"Well," said Neil, "she's had a long day and she's not really feeling up to it and-"

"Sorry," said Macleod, " but, Neil, I have a murder investigation on and Miss Haskins is my first visit. There shall be many more visits tonight to others involved in this situation so forgive me if I insist on Miss Haskins' cooperation. Tomorrow just won't do." Turning to Georgie Haskins, Macleod smiled and simply asked, "Can you run through exactly what happened to you today and what you saw? In your own words and time, please. Thank you."

Macleod listened impassively as the woman told her tale, sniffing her way through most of it and giving long pauses when describing what she had seen inside the bothy. Part of him felt an empathy for her, as no one should ever have to come across something like that, but inside the detective was thinking hard, looking for what he needed to know, even if it was not apparent yet.

"When you saw the heads of the victims, Miss Haskins, did you see anything inside the mouths?" asked Macleod.

"I really didn't hang about for an inspection."

"Indeed no, I wasn't asking if you touched them or examined them, but, please, this is important. Did you see anything in the mouths as you glanced at the heads? It would maybe only have been a glimpse, but if you can try to remember, take yourself through the sweep of your eyes."

Georgie Haskins began to cry again and her partner leaned forward and held her. "Really Inspector, is this really necessary?"

"Yes, sir, it is," said Macleod in his matter-of-fact voice. "Miss Haskins, anything? Did you see anything?"

Miss Haskins sniffed and then blurted out something unintelligible.

"Sorry but I didn't catch that," said Macleod. "What did you say?"

"Scroll. Like a small scroll, I think. Maybe a roll-up. Was only a … glimpse. The head … and the body … oh God."

"Sorry to press, Miss Haskins, focus on the scroll, what colour was it? Size? Could you tell if anything was written on it?"

"Small, it was small, like a cigarette. But not white. A sandy colour, I think, yes, sandy, like dark sand. Not the bright beach type, the wet stuff, like that."

"Was it wet?"

"Don't think so. It was only a glance and then I ran, to get your people."

"You did well," said Hope, "really well. One more thing though. Did you smell anything in the bothy?"

Macleod watched the woman think back and then grab her

nose. "The stench, foul, corrupt, like rotting bins but worse, more like … rotting flesh maybe. I think so. Maybe, I don't recall. Sorry, I don't know."

"Any smell of fuel, Miss Haskins, like you would get at a petrol pump, or diesel?" asked Macleod.

"No, I don't recall that. I was so surprised when it all went on fire. I would have thought about that if there had been fuel, surely. No?"

"Maybe," said Macleod. "Thank you for your assistance today, I'm sorry you had to see that, but you've been a great help. I don't know if there will be much else from us, but if so, we will get in touch. Please don't discuss these details you mentioned outside of this room, it could compromise the investigation."

"Of course she won't," said Neil.

"And neither must you, sir. No ill-advised comments to any strangers." Macleod watched the man squirm and then left on his heel.

"What was that all about?" asked Hope as they walked back along the ward corridor. "You were a bit harsh on the partner there."

"Just giving him a warning."

"Why, you think he'll talk to the press?"

"Maybe, I don't know. But what I do know is he likes to pick out women and make comments to awaiting policemen in hospital shops. And in case you ever worry about your figure, McGrath, you're a right wee bit of stuff."

Hope rolled her eyes and Macleod laughed. Together they walked out of the hospital and into the dark night that had descended on Inverness. Macleod had asked Ross to make sure the head of the radio station was there to see him on arrival.

But he was hungry and he directed Hope to take him to the large supermarket in the town. Impatient with the service of the cafe inside, Macleod went up twice to get their food hurried up and Hope rebuked him saying she doubted he could make an omelette in the time he was demanding fish and chips.

Once the quick dinner was had, they made their way to the radio station and Macleod sent Hope on ahead, saying he would follow shortly. Once she was on her way from the car, he took his mobile phone and rang a number. There was an answer message coming on immediately. *Blast it,* he thought, *if I don't get her now, I'll not get a chance until after midnight.*

Macleod had never been to a radio station and so the building in front of him was rather disappointing. He had imagined a grand front and an old-style architectural masterpiece but, then again, maybe the London BBC office was not common to all broadcasters. The building itself was rather dull, grey, with just a single "Monster" logo on the outside.

A girl at the reception desk grabbed Macleod as he walked in and directed him towards an office at the end of a long corridor. On opening, the door revealed a middle-aged woman sitting in a smart blouse with auburn hair that flowed around her head like bubbles of shampoo that had gotten out of control. As she saw him enter she came round from behind the desk and extended a hand. Hope was already in the office.

"Inspector, your colleague has already advised you were coming. My name is Laura Tulloch, station general manager. I'm at your disposal. Can I get you a coffee or anything?"

"No, thank you," said Macleod. "I'd like to know about your missing DJ."

"You think he's in the bothy on the Black Isle, don't you?"

"At this time enquiries are continuing, but we know that

your colleague is missing and that's giving us concern. As such we need to ascertain if anything is up with him."

"What do you know of his movements yesterday?" asked Hope, speaking from the side of the room where Macleod saw her installed on a low sofa.

"He came in for his morning show, everything seemed normal. Andy was pretty old school in that he ran in the door just beforehand and then would produce a bit of magic on air. His producer selected all the music, but Andy had a rapport with the listener second to none."

"And that's Andy *Howling* MacTavish. The report said he was forty. Bit young for old school."

"Well, yes, but that's how he was. In saying that, I think our audience has moved due to the younger shows we are putting on during the rest of the day, aimed more at the teens to twenties, I'm afraid. His ratings were dropping pretty steeply."

"And I take it that caused you a problem. Why not simply replace him?" asked Hope.

"Well, he has a water-tight contract that states we can't. Signed by an old station manager buddy of his. I offered good money for him to go, but I think he just likes the adulation of an audience every day, even if they are dwindling."

"And so was he here for long yesterday?" asked Macleod.

"Disappeared about three I think, right after a bit of argy-bargy with *Gen* Mochilas. Not sure what that was about but it seemed kind of heated. Jimmy's desperate for that morning slot. Young man of thirty with a lot of potential. It should really be him up there. He's got a better rapport with the kids. More street as they say."

"I'm sure they do," muttered Macleod. "So this Gen, or is it Jimmy?"

"Jimmy *The Gen* Mochilas. They have to have stupid names. Trust me, Inspector, I know. Ego-driven sods the lot of them, it's like looking after babies, it really is. But without them I don't have any shows."

"So was this Jimmy meant to be in at that time?"

"No, he usually comes in at seven for his show. In fact, I'm not sure why he was here at all."

"If you can give Detective McGrath the address of Jimmy or Gen or whatever he's called, she can pop round for a word tonight, clear up a few things. Have you heard from MacTavish's wife?"

"No Inspector, not directly. Anna, my receptionist, gave her a call this morning when he didn't turn up for his show. He was already late then by about two hours. To be honest, I don't think his wife gives a damn about him. You see, Inspector, MacTavish hits the bottle hard and possibly his women harder. He's a damn liability for me, but thank God I don't have to live with him."

Macleod bit his lip. Something wasn't right here. All too simple. He might be over a cliff on the road, in a ditch, something like that. But the murder that had taken place, if that was him, it wasn't something that happened to a man who was simply off the rails. No, he would have provoked someone pretty hard.

"Well Miss Tulloch, I think that's it, except to give you my card. If you hear from him or think of anything else relevant, simply call me. And thank you for hanging back to see me. Let's hope it's not your man in the tragedy at the bothy."

"Indeed Inspector, although would solve my problems if it were."

*Indeed it would,* thought Macleod, *way too easily*. She wasn't hiding the fact, but then again, maybe that was a bluff too. He heard the station manager call the receptionist, asking her to escort the visitors out and the young girl at the desk promptly entered the room.

"Oh, and the address, please" said Hope to the manager.

"Just ask Miss Campbell, she's very efficient."

As they walked back to the reception desk, Macleod asked Hope to go to Mochilas' address after dropping him off at the MacTavish house.

"I want to see this wife for myself. But you can handle Mochilas. Find out if he's the murdering type. I'd say he has a reason but it depends on his temperament."

"Yes, sir. Oh, and by the way, did you get her?"

"Who?"

"Your bed warmer."

*Anyone else and I'd have snapped at them*, thought Macleod. "Enough Detective, that's enough."

# Chapter 5

Hope watched Macleod walk out of the radio station while she headed to the receptionist. The girl seemed engaging enough and, when asked to provide Hope with an address for Jimmy Mochilas, instantly delved into the computer on her desk. Within a minute, she had written it out long hand and handed it to Hope.

"Do you mind me asking you something?" said the girl on letting go of the note.

"Never minded someone asking. Whether or not I am at liberty to reply is another issue, but please ask away."

"It's just that … is it Andy out there?"

"I'm not at liberty to answer that and especially to a media outlet," said Hope, smiling. "I appreciate you'll be quite worried about him here, but I can't say anything about that question at the moment."

"We won't all be worried," said the girl in a hushed tone.

"I'm sorry?" queried Hope. "What did you say?"

"Not all of us will be so worried. Not about Andy."

"Do you want to tell me something?"

The girl shook her head. "Not here. Definitely not here."

"Okay, I've got to run my boss to another address and then I have something to do myself, but do you need a lift home?"

The door down the corridor opened and the station manager walked out in a long plush coat complete with high heels. She had an elegant stride, powerful but sophisticated, and Hope saw someone clearly in charge, or at least who thought they were.

"Did you get the detective what she needed, Anna?"

"Yes, she did," said Hope. "Thank you."

"Good," said Laura Tulloch. "I am heading out to meet a friend and I'm late so can you just close up my office, Anna, and then get off home yourself. You've been a great help today."

"It's fine, Miss Tulloch. Let's hope they find him safe and well," said Anna.

"Of course. I'm sure they will. But I think Jimmy can cover the show tomorrow whatever. Anyway, good night Anna. Also to you, Detective. If you need anything else from me just call."

With that the manager swept out of the building where she gave a cheery goodbye to Macleod. Hope turned back to Anna but she had already started putting her coat on as she hurried down the hallway to the manager's office, which she promptly locked. A minute later the girl was stood at her desk, eyes looking out of the window.

"So do you need a lift?" asked Hope again.

"Yes, but wait 'til the bitch is gone. Don't want her to see you taking me home."

"Why? Is she involved?"

"I didn't say that. So it is Andy out there?"

"And I didn't say that either," snapped Hope. "As my boss would say, investigations are ongoing. That's her car away," she indicated, backing it up with a finger pointed to the car park, "so get your stuff. I think I want to hear what you have to say."

"Okay, but only you, not your boss."

"Why the hell not?"

"Don't like bosses and I don't like men who think they are in charge either."

Hope wondered what the statement was all about, but she was not going to stop a potential informant from talking simply to defend her boss' reputation to a girl, one who did not even know him. They walked out of the station together and Hope shouted to Macleod who had taken a walk to the edge of the car park. He was taking in the view of Inverness.

"I'm going to drop you off and then give Anna here a lift home." Hope saw Macleod nod and then usher the girl towards the car. Once she was inside and the door was closed, Macleod came round to the driver's side and whispered in Hope's ear.

"Information?"

"Yes," replied Hope, "but she doesn't want you there."

"You okay with that?"

"Yeah, fine. Anyway what's happening with the bed warmer?"

"Shut up, Hope."

The drive to the home of the MacTavishes was a short one and was easily identifiable by the police car outside. There was a press scrum there too. Hope dropped Macleod short of everyone and watched him approach the press as if he was simply going to walk right past them and continue along the road. At the last moment, he pulled his ID and placed it before the officer on duty before quickly hurrying inside. *God, he's an old pro,* thought Hope.

"Do you like coffee?" asked Hope.

"No, but I do like frappuccinos," replied Anna.

"Okay, tell me where's good and near and we'll get some.

Then we'll have a chat somewhere else."

After driving to a nearby coffee shop and paying what Hope thought was an extortionate price for two drinks, she drove off until she spied a car park overlooking Inverness. It was deserted, and parking at the furthest point from the road Hope indicated they should get out. Taking her leather jacket from the boot and a black bobble hat, she then sat on the bonnet, waiting for Anna to join her.

"Okay then," said Hope, "what did you want to say back at the station?"

"Well, that nice, friendly station act for one. That's a load of shit. She couldn't give a crap about Andy, she wants him out. But they can't because he has a contract."

"Well," said Hope, "so far you've told me what your manager told me already. She wants him off the show, says he's not up to it, ratings and that."

"She would say that. Andy's the best, but they cut his budget, made him change his jingles and dropped some of his competitions. She's doing everything to move him out, but she can't. And then there's Jimmy. Bloody vulture. Can't wait to put the boot in. Came over today and gave Andy some agro about something stupid. I tell you those two would stop at nothing. Andy's a peach, possibly the sweetest guy I've met. And they just want rid of him."

"That's not the view that everyone has though. I thought he hit the bottle, was a bit of a pisshead."

"Hang on a minute," spat Anna, "that's bullshit. Yeah, he likes his drink and that, but the few times he's overdone it was their fault. He's been under a lot of pressure. Beneath it all he's very caring, a very passionate guy. Eloquent and sensitive. Very gentle."

Hope could see Anna held a fondness that didn't speak of a colleague but something more. Deciding to go for the jugular, she got off the bonnet and turned to look directly at Anna. "Were you two an item? Like an under-the-covers item?"

The blush came immediately, and, try as she might to cover it up, Anna struggled. "Item? I wish we were an item. Andy's too much of a free spirit to be an item."

"So he shags about then?"

The girl looked up at Hope and she thought she saw a tear in her eye. "Yes, he shags about. Says he has a lot of love to give."

"And you were one of his loves. Still the case or has he moved on to someone else?"

The girl hung her head. "He's still with me, but we have an open relationship."

"Is he seeing anyone else of note at the station?" Anna shook her head. "Anyone else you know?"

"Yeah, he's been with two of my friends. Sarah and Lib."

"They both from round here?"

"No. Sarah's the other side of Inverness and Lib's on the Black Isle."

The hairs on Hope's neck pricked up and she had a sick feeling in her stomach about Anna's friends. "I'm going to need addresses for them."

"No way, I'm telling you this in confidence. This is about those people getting after Andy."

"I'm afraid not. I need their addresses. We found two bodies at the bothy. One of those bodies is a young woman, about your age, certainly that range."

"Well, it's not Sarah, she texted me this afternoon. Can't do that when you're dead."

"And Lib?" prompted Hope.

"Doesn't have a telephone or a mobile. At least not one she can answer."

"How come?"

"Father doesn't allow her one. And she doesn't get to answer the household one. So she never gave me it. In fact, I've never been to her house. It's on the Black Isle beyond Rosemarkie."

Hope went back inside the car and then placed a map in front of Anna. "Where on the Black Isle?" Anna pointed to a house midway between Cromarty and Rosemarkie. "Okay, I need to drop you off at home, but I might need to talk to you again."

"Do you think she's involved? I doubt it. Her father would never have let her out for a start. Controlling git. It won't be her."

"All the same I have to be sure. Not a word to anyone. If the press get anything from you I'll come looking. Now, drink up and get in."

# Chapter 6

Macleod walked through the front door of what was a reasonably middle-class house. The hallway was neat with some photographs on the wall, showing smiling faces and even some awards. But there were no children. *Typical cop,* he thought, *always looking for what's wrong. Not that not having kids is wrong, just seen too many marriages under stress because of the issue of non-conception. We never had.*

His mind was brought back into order by a door opening in front of him and a female constable looked at him blankly. Macleod held up his ID and smiled.

"Sorry sir, didn't recognise you. She's just in here," said the woman, pointing to the door she had only recently opened.

"Not been up here, Constable, so not your fault. How's she been?"

"Worked up. Trying to keep a brave face on it, but she knows we've found something up at the bothy."

"Okay, stay close, just in case she gets too worked up. I don't have the female touch."

"Not many women do either, sir," came the quip back. Somehow he had said something offensive. *But I was being complimentary,* thought Macleod. *Women are more compassion-*

*ate, on the whole, better at getting alongside. I can't fathom today's ways, you can't say anything.*

He entered the lounge, which he noted had a soft plush carpet, the kind of thing you could comfortably lie down on. The sofa was leather, cream in colour, and around the room were several cushions and knickknacks. *How did Jane put it? The room was dressed. How do you ever dress a room? Madness.*

On one of the single chairs of the sofa was a woman dressed in a pair of designer jeans and a beige jumper that fitted her perfectly. She was probably mid-forties, had immaculate hair and the perfume she wore dominated the room. It was designed to be engaging, but Macleod found it to be cloying. But, then again, he had never understood perfume. The smell of a woman was enough, no additions were needed. Although old body odour did require a shower.

"Sorry to disturb you, Mrs MacTavish, but I'm Detective Inspector Macleod and I'm taking over this case so I'll need to run through a few things with you."

"Is he in that dammed bothy?" the woman snapped. "Tell me, I have a right to know."

"Indeed you do, and the moment I can confirm the identity of the body in the building I will let you know. Until then, I need to track your husband's movements." Macleod watched the woman back down and sink into the chair. "Now, he was at the radio station yesterday, left about three. Did you hear or see him after that?"

"Yes, I told your people. He popped back briefly, told me he wasn't going to be here for dinner and pissed off out."

"And when was this?"

"About five o'clock. I hadn't made any dinner anyway so it was no big deal."

Macleod furrowed the skin above his eyes. "Weren't you expecting to eat together?"

The woman laughed. "That wee bastard hasn't eaten dinner with me more than twice in the last month. There's only one thing that's been driving that man and it's the same thing that's been driving him these last twenty years of marriage. It swings between his legs, does all the thinking and gets unsuspecting girls into trouble."

"So he played around," said Macleod flatly.

"No, he played at home. That was the exception. His waving his dick at any bit of skirt that came past him was just normal practice. Look at me, Inspector, I married a shit. You understand, a dirty-minded wee shit."

Macleod sat down on the largest piece of the sofa and tried to stop himself falling back comically, knowing at this time it would be wholly inappropriate. "Perhaps the Constable could kindly get us a tea or something."

"And what? Just calm us all down?"

"Mrs MacTavish, you are obviously angry, worried and probably scared. That's perfectly fine, but I need to trace your husband whether in a ditch, in a car or whether his *dicking about,* as you put it, has finally caught up with him. To do that I need you calm, okay? Then we might get some answers and find him. Your anger is understandable, but frankly it is not useful at this time."

The woman glowered at him but then sunk back down into the chair. "Okay, okay. Tea, I'll take tea. Top cupboard, none of the cheap shit I give to guests."

"Good," said Macleod, giving a nod to the constable to get busy with the drinks. "Coffee, thanks." As the officer walked off, Macleod stared at the woman. Her eyes were wet and the mascara had run causing her face to look like she was ready for the lights of an American football match rather than receiving guests.

"So, he left here at five and then there's been no contact."

"That's right. I did ring him at eleven last night to tell him I was off to bed and that he'd better not disturb me. At least the wee shit didn't do that."

"How many years married?" asked Macleod.

"Twenty, two months ago. He was only twenty and I was twenty-five, but he had the gift of the gab. That's his skill, Detective, he can engage you from the first moment and you don't notice the time pass until he's left the room. It's why he managed to do the radio job. It's why the previous boss wanted him. I made him get a good contract. It's why we still have all this."

Macleod forced himself to lie back gently on the sofa. "So why does he play about? You have a great house and I imagine you could afford to keep yourselves entertained and busy. So what's the issue?"

"He's infertile. We found out four years after being together. And that's when he started seeing other women. At first, I think it was to prove he wasn't infertile and it was me. But now it's because he can't stop his dick from wandering. It's also what started the drinking."

"Heavy on it, is he?"

"Amazingly so. But able to hold it to a point. That's a point that you or I would collapse from. But anymore and he goes daft."

"Violent?"

"Never. He does actually treat a woman well if he's with her. It's just when he leaves he becomes a shit."

The constable entered the room and Macleod watched Mrs MacTavish take her tea with two hands. The saucer shook causing the tea to spill a little.

"Ever contemplate a divorce?" asked Macleod.

"Contemplate?" she said, raising her voice. "I begged him, but he wouldn't have it. See those wee bitches wouldn't cook or clean for him, run his house for him. And he knows that."

"Any ideas who he was after at the moment?"

"That receptionist in the station. Caught him looking at her in a bikini in her Facebook holiday pics and he was sat there, just drooling. Didn't even see me looking over his shoulder. Doing it in our house too, brazen bastard. Do you know how that makes me feel? I ain't done, Inspector, I would have happily let him be with me. Do I look that bad?"

Macleod wondered if she wanted the answer. Of course she didn't look bad, but she had aged. He had, we all did. But the receptionist was not yet aging in the bad way; in fact, she had probably reached her prime, about twenty-five. That's if all you did was see the outside. Not knowing what answer was expected, or if any would be accepted as truthful that didn't hurt, Macleod kept quiet.

"I thought when he went out he had aftershave on. He hadn't shaved, just splashed it on. Frankly I didn't care, he was always shagging around. I'm a fool still being here, aren't I? I hope the bastard's dead."

And then she began to cry, her head going to her hands. The shoulders shook and the tea was dropped, splashing over the carpet. "Shit, bloody shit."

"Constable, a cloth and get that cleared up, please." The officer leapt into action and Macleod sat there and studied his witness. She looked genuine and maybe she was. You can still cry over the victim when you've killed them.

"Where were you last night, Mrs MacTavish?" He saw angry eyes raise to him. "Purely routine, we need to eliminate you from enquiries."

"Here, on my own. *Corrie*, some stupid show, a Christmas movie on one of the channels you only surf to. And then bed, alone, like every night for the last fifteen years. He only ever came in when he couldn't get it anywhere else."

*No alibi*, thought Macleod, *and she's definitely a suspect. I'll need to check the neighbours and car movements.*

"What's your husband's car?"

"White Audi. I told your other lackeys."

"And your car?"

"I can't drive. Never have."

"So the one in the drive is his then?"

Mrs MacTavish tutted. "What the hell do you think? I said I didn't drive."

"Why didn't he take it?"

"Probably pissed. He's been caught plenty in the past so these days he takes taxis."

Macleod stood up. "Thank you for your time. There may be more and I'll keep you informed if we find anything. He watched the woman nod and then put her head in her hands again. Turning away, Macleod listened to her sobbing. "One more thing. Have you ever been to that bothy?"

The woman looked up, her eyes red and the tears still falling. "Yes! It was where we first got it together. It was my place, where we did it. But he couldn't even let me keep that."

Macleod nodded and then indicated the constable should attend to Mrs MacTavish. *Life got complicated around showbiz people. Maybe it was the fame.*

Exiting the room, Macleod found one of the other uniformed police officers. Taking him through to the kitchen, he ran through the actions taken.

"Anything from the neighbours?"

"Yes sir," said the young constable. "We have him sighted coming home yesterday not long after three. Then he leaves later in a taxi. We're chasing that company up at this time."

"And it's five o'clock for leaving?"

"Yes sir. Apparently, he seemed his normal self on the way out to the taxi, nothing unusual."

"Clothing?"

"Dark jeans, shirt and a large coat. Gloves too."

"Expecting the cold then. Okay, well done, if there's anything else send it via the station until we set up the incident room." Macleod turned and walked back into the hallway and began to study the photographs on the wall. It seemed the DJ was quite a star over the years in this part of the country and there were awards galore. His mobile rang and he saw a new number.

"Yes, Macleod."

"Good evening sir, it's Ross. It's getting dark out here and most of us will be retiring to Cromarty to get the incident room set up. It's in the town hall, beside the football pitch. Probably the nearest place with a kitchen and other facilities. There's a guest house in the town I'm going to book you and the DC into, if that's fine with you. It's clean and flexible with you coming and going."

"Yes, that's all fine, Ross, whatever works. I'll be heading your way presently and you can call the troops together for eight o'clock. McGrath will give the briefing. Anything further from forensics?"

"Not yet."

"Fine," said Macleod, "see you at eight." Hanging up in his usual brisk manner, he heard some commotion outside. Opening the front door, he saw someone trying to break the line of press and being bombarded with questions. On further inspection he saw it was Laura Tulloch, dressed in a long fur coat . As she was escorted through by the uniformed officer at the front, she stumbled and Macleod saw she was wearing tall stilettoes.

Miss Tulloch, this way please," shouted Macleod, indicating he would take it from here to the uniformed officer,

"Thank you, Inspector, it's really quite a scrum out here."

Cameras clicked and flashes nearly blinded Macleod as he took Miss Tulloch's hand and escorted her to the front door. "I take it this is a social visit, see how the troubled wife is?"

"Exactly Inspector, one has to look after the radio family despite being on an engagement."

"Fine," he replied indolently, and then rapped the door. The female officer opened it and, on being informed of the visitor, hurried off to the living room to advise Mrs MacTavish. Macleod heard something smash on the floor and then there was a thump and the living room door opened wide, clattering into the wall.

"Get that bitch out of here. You hounded him, you bloody hounded him with your contract. That bottle grew when you arrived and he went right to the bottom of it. Come here, you cow."

Macleod stepped forward to place himself between the warring women but received a punch to the nose for his troubles. More cameras clicked and his mobile went off in his pocket. Ignoring it, he tried to grab Mrs MacTavish's hands, but she was now kicking out and he caught a blow on the shin causing him to bend down. Glancing up, he saw one set of female hands on the head of the other and hair was being pulled. As he went to get back up, another foot caught him right between the legs. He doubled up and fell over.

"Back, get back or I'll book you for obstruction and no more cameras. That means you. I see you."

It was Hope's voice and Macleod smiled.

"You, the blonde, get inside with the officer and you, ma'am, are coming inside with me."

Standing up, Macleod watched McGrath grab Mrs MacTavish and place an arm behind her back forcing her inside. The female officer then escorted Laura Tulloch inside as well, leaving Macleod alone with the uniformed male officer outside and a horde of now very happy press.

"And you lot, back to the street," said Macleod. "Show's over. Back you go."

"Hope your bollocks get better."

If Macleod had seen who said it he would have gone for him, but there had been enough entertainment. Making sure the press had retreated, he made his way inside still feeling like he was missing something between his legs. *Heck, that's so sore, right on the money.*

As he entered the hallway, he saw Hope coming out of the kitchen. "This can wait, sir, Henderson has her in the kitchen and he'll let her out in a few minutes via the back way to a taxi. Our other officer has the wife seated again."

"Good," said Macleod, "but what's up?"

"I have a name and it might be attached to the girl's body in the bothy. We need to see her family now."

# Chapter 7

It was a good half hour to the location that had been given and, with night having fallen, Hope found herself having to focus hard on the road, the early start beginning to catch up. On the way over, she briefed her boss on the information she had obtained from Anna Campbell and ignored his horrified look when she used the word "shagging". His distain for the whole romantic life of the station was evident and, to be fair, she was not that comfortable with it either.

The car weaved along a single-track road until it came upon a gateway with a large white sign on it. "Carlton farm: Private Property. Any intrusion will be dealt with by force."

"That's an interesting take," said Hope.

"Just keep your wits about you. And don't get out of the car too quickly," advised Macleod before stepping out and opening the gate. He pulled it back and let Hope bring the car on before closing it behind him. The road was now a dirt track with a few stones thrown down here and there in patches, presumably where the potholes kept coming back over time. After a short drive, a large house appeared with only a few lights on.

Hope rolled the car to a halt outside the front door and Macleod saw it open. The end of a shotgun emerged and

Macleod indicated the issue to Hope. "Stay here. Be ready to call for backup."

Opening the door slowly, Macleod stepped out and stood facing the door. "Police! This is the police! Lower the shotgun or you may be breaking the law by threatening a police officer."

"What the hell do you want? We got nothing here for you scum. Nothing, you hear. Now piss off!"

The voice was deep and gravelly and Macleod imagined an older man with scars. Maybe the detective programmes on the telly were getting to him. But the shotgun was still raised.

"Do you have a licence for that weapon, sir? I suggest you lower it or I will be forced to come with other officers to check the legality of that weapon. And if it's still pointed at us then they will take action you won't like."

"Told you. We got nothing here for you. Now piss off, pig, leave a man to his own devices. You wankers are the state's damn lackeys."

Macleod stepped out from behind the car door and watched the weapon remain trained on him. "I'm investigating a murder and I need information, which only you can give me, so put down the weapon."

"You think it was us. Why? Just because we keep to ourselves. Well, I ain't done nothing, I ain't been to that bothy on the news."

Macleod was getting annoyed now. The gun was still trained on him and he was beginning to worry that this situation might go south. "I was going to ask this inside, sir, but where is your daughter? Is your daughter at home?"

"Which one?"

"Lib, Lib Carlton, sir. I take it you are Mr Carlton?"

The gun lowered and the door opened. A man with a grey

beard and a stooped disposition limped forward. His eyes had large rings around them.

"What about our Liberty? You better not be saying she was committing murder or I'll ring your neck for such a suggestion. My girls are all good ones. Love their daddy and keep this place in order. Make a man a good wife one day she will. Loyal, giving, listen to her husband and provide for him. I'll have nothing said about her, you understand!"

Macleod stepped forward and the gun was raised up again. He swallowed hard but continued forward. "Where is she? I have concerns for her welfare."

"Well, you don't need to, sir. You can just take your hide back out of here and piss off. We're fine." The man spat on the ground and flicked the shotgun and indicated that Macleod should leave or face the consequences.

"No. I'm here from the police and I need to satisfy myself that your daughter is safe and well. Bring her out here and show me that and I'll go. Stall me any further and I'll bring a lot more people and ask a heck of a lot more questions. Could be pretty invasive. Understand me. I won't do any more than is warranted but I will do *everything* that is."

"Curse you. Damn pig." The man lowered the weapon and turned back to the house. "Precious, get Liberty out here." The man turned back to Macleod and stared at him. In the silence the men glowered at each other and Macleod sought to see what was behind the man's front.

A women leaned out of the door, only her head and shoulders showing. "I can't find her, sir, she's not there. Her bed's not been slept in."

The man spun round and marched towards the woman. "What the blazes are you saying? Was she not here tonight?

Sera said she was not feeling well, said her sister was sick. Did she lie to me? I'll beat that girl."

"Enough!" shouted Macleod. "Is she missing? Ma'am, I'm with the police, Detective Inspector Macleod, is Liberty missing?"

"The police," screamed the woman and ran out of the front door towards Macleod. She was in a flimsy long T-shirt and came forward hysterically only to be grabbed by the man.

"What are you doing, woman? Get back inside and stop showing yourself to that pig. Get inside and get covered up."

"Lib? Where's Lib?" She continued to scream and the man pushed her back. Suddenly a younger woman ran out in a negligee. The man yelled at the new arrival who ran to the older woman. Without hesitation the man swung his arm and struck the girl across the face, flooring her. Hope was out of the car in an instant.

"Enough!" shouted Macleod again and ran at the man whilst wary of the shotgun. He saw it begin to rise and grabbed it as Hope arrived and took the man's wrist, driving it behind his back, freeing the woman in the process.

"Where's Liberty?" yelled the older woman.

"Get your bitch's hands off me. I ain't being held by no slut."

"Enough!" shouted Macleod again, opening the shotgun and emptying the cartridges. "We are going inside where we will discuss this. Ma'am, take the young girl inside and both kindly put something more substantial on. I will then talk to you. McGrath, cuff this one and take him inside. And if he calls you a slut again, or even a bitch, book him and take him down the station to the cells. We'll leave him there until he learns how to treat a woman."

"I'll treat my girls how I like, they're mine, I own them. This is my land and my home. I'll decide what goes down." The man struggled as Hope placed handcuffs on him. She pushed him up towards a wall and worked the cuffs onto the wrists. As she had just finished, she saw something in the dark, a change of tone. Something burst from the perimeter into the light of the doorway and she saw it run towards Macleod.

"Sir!" yelled Hope.

Macleod was trying to usher the woman inside when he heard the warning. Something came at him from his side and he stepped backwards leaving a single foot outstretched. Someone large, built like a brick house and with youthful flowing blond hair, caught Macleod's foot and fell face first to the ground. Years of experience told Macleod not to wait and he drove a knee into the back of the man and grabbed the wrists, taking them behind him. He whipped his own cuffs out and secured his attacker.

"Don't hurt him," screamed the woman. "Don't hurt my Ven."

"He's going to be charged with assault. Now, let's get inside and calm down," said Macleod. "There's a missing girl and we need to find her, so kindly behave. McGrath, when we're inside and calmed down, ring the team and get some people out here. We're going to need to have a liaison and some uniforms to keep the peace."

Hope nodded and marched the father inside while Macleod lifted his attacker to his feet and followed. The mother wept as she tailed Macleod, begging him for information.

"Where is she? What's happened? Is it to do with the bothy, is she in the bothy?"

The woman wailed and Macleod asked her to come inside. On entering a hallway, his attacker before him, he followed Hope into a lounge with two large armchairs and some small pouffe seats. They manhandled their charges into the armchairs, hands still cuffed behind them, and Macleod turned to the mother and the young girl.

"Go and put something else on, please. That's a bit flimsy for a house that's about to have a number of officers in here."

"You have Papa in the wrong chair," said the girl. "Papa's in Ven's chair and Ven's in Papa's."

Macleod looked at her strangely. "So where do you sit?"

"On the small ones, with Mama and Lib. And there's Missy's chair."

"Don't say that ill-disciplined, ungrateful bitch's name," yelled the father.

"You! Shut it!" Hope said firmly.

"I don't take no orders from no girl."

"You'll take orders from whoever gives them from my unit and start showing some respect to my female officer." Macleod watched the man spit on the floor. "Ladies, get upstairs, please, and get something more substantial on as asked." Macleod saw the women look to the father.

"You see, Detective, they know their place. A woman is the more attractive of the species, should be able to show her feathers all the time. But you're right, not before strangers, go on, Mama."

Macleod thought he was going to turn sick at the voice and implications being bandied, but his real concern was that Hope didn't simply punch the man. Or worse, castrate him! "Detective McGrath, kindly escort the ladies upstairs and insist they dress appropriately. And McGrath," said Macleod, pulling her close to whisper, "find out what the hell's going on in this family."

Hope nodded and ushered the women from the room.

Macleod heard her calling the station and then focused on his two handcuffed men in the armchairs.

"I have a nightstick on me," said Macleod, "and any further attack on me will be met with force. I like my shape and figure, and I like it intact so I don't tend to wait when being attacked. So sit there, don't move and answer my questions. Have you a photograph of your daughter?"

"Family picture over the mantelpiece. She's the one in my arms," the father said.

Macleod turned halfway around, keeping an eye on the men. From the corner of his vision he saw a family grouped, the women in the front and the father and son behind them. The women were dressed up in old-fashioned clothes that covered them from the neck to the ankle, a complete change from how they were dressed when he arrived. But one of the daughters' faces was blacked out.

"I take it that's Missy that's been erased."

"She ain't no part of this family!" spat the man.

While interested in what had happened to cause this reaction, Macleod decided that Liberty needed to be his main focus. "And Liberty, where do you think she is?"

The man grunted and looked away, but Macleod saw the young man stare at him. Raising his eyebrows, Macleod invited a comment and he could see the man start to speak but then look at his father.

"Just say it," advised Macleod. "If you don't say it here, we can discuss it at the station."

"She's gone wrong, Papa said so, said she needed dealt with because she's not behaving. Doesn't know her place."

"Indeed," said Macleod, "in what way?"

"I think the girl has been itching to see someone," said Mr

Carlton. "That girl from the radio station that caused it, putting ideas in her head. It's not right for a girl to disobey her father, with her magazines, lusting after some man. I knows what's best for them, who's best for them. Don't need no interference."

"Where have you been today, sir, and last night?"

"On the farm, so has Ven. No one left. All of us been here for the last three days."

"Except Liberty, she's somewhere else," said Macleod. "You are both going down the station and I'm going to check whether you have a licence for that firearm. Either way, you're going to be cautioned. Meanwhile I shall try to find your daughter." Macleod looked at the photo again. "Do you have a regular dentist?"

"Aye, why?"

"Who is it?" asked Macleod.

"Mama will have it," said the older man. *Dental records probably the best bet for a quick ID,* thought Macleod, *but how do you tell that to a mother?*

# Chapter 8

Hope followed the women upstairs to a landing where they parted company, the mother taking the door on the left and the daughter continuing to a room on the right. Questions needed to be answered, but Hope kept her curiosity in abeyance while the mother was going to change. As she looked around the landing, she saw a number of photographs and in over half of them someone, a girl, had her face blanked out by black marker.

"Unusual to keep pictures up when you clearly have someone you don't want in them."

"What's that? You can come in and talk to me, Papa's not in here, it's fine," said the mother from inside the room.

"I said strange to have photos up with someone you don't want in them."

"Papa don't like to be reminded about our disappointment," said the mother coolly. "But she's still my blood. He lets me keep her on the wall as long as he doesn't have to look at her."

About to answer and point out the absurdity of the statement, Hope decided instead to try to reach the woman. "What's your name?"

"I'm Mama, and down the corridor is Sera. She's my second. The one on the wall is Missy. She has great looks, don't you think?"

Hope coughed. "Not sure the photo does her justice. What's your full name, Mama?"

"Oh, no one calls me by that."

"Let me, please."

The woman dropped her gown and Hope turned away slightly at her naked figure to try to show some decency. But a red mark on the rear of the left thigh caught her eye. It looked thin and painful, but the woman was paying it no heed as she walked to a wardrobe and pulled out a long dress. *Quite frumpy,* thought Hope, *not like the gown.*

"I'm Mrs Carlton, Precious Carlton, and the man downstairs is Justin Carlton who I married over 20 years ago. He was a catch, an older man with prospects as my father said. And in the Louisiana sun, he simply looked stunning."

There was something of an unreality to the conversation and Hope tried to picture the man downstairs in younger days, but she could not manage a *stunning* aspect. "Who's your son?"

"That's Ven, he's a good boy, looks after us along with Papa. You don't go wrong with good men like that around."

Something struck Hope. "Louisiana sun? Where you in America then? Is that where you come from?"

The woman shook her head and asked Hope to fix up her back. "No, I come from round here, but I met Justin here and my parents did not approve. We ran off to America and found Winston and his followers and were lucky enough to get a place in his compound. Got married there not long after my nineteenth birthday. Had my first not long after."

"Okay, so all the kids born there?"

"Yes, all of them, but we had to leave and come back to Scotland after Sera was born."

Hope took the back of the woman's dress and went to attach the fixings but then something caught her breath. She had not been looking at the woman since she saw the thigh injury, but now looking at her back, she saw the lace bra. Further down was a thong and possibly hold-ups. While Hope had nothing against exciting underwear, it was at odds with the rather drab dress that seemed to be designed to package a whole woman without letting anything show.

"Why did you have to leave?" asked Hope.

"The compound was burnt down. Some people didn't like our happiness. Nastiness in the world, Detective."

"I had noticed, what with my job, but didn't you report it to the authorities? You shouldn't have to suffer abuse like that."

The woman shook her head as Hope fastened the last fixture. "That's Papa's domain. I have the kids to raise, the house to keep and Papa to keep satisfied. He takes care of the outside things."

Something was not right with the setup and, as much as Hope was into alternative lifestyles, she struggled not to see this one as abusive. "Does Papa keep a tight rein on the kids?"

"Papa keeps a tight rein on us all, but then he has so much to do, so much responsibility. That's a man's place, is it not? Are you married, Detective?"

"No, not sure I've found a man who can handle me." Hope grinned. *Or even a woman.* "So where would your daughter go? Does Liberty have any friends?"

"She has a few from the school. Papa wasn't keen, but she was allowed out on occasion with them. Do you think she could be with them? It would be unusual. She often goes for a walk to the beach, but Papa had told her to stay in last night and she wouldn't disobey Papa."

"And yet she's gone. What are the names of these friends? And do you have contacts for them?"

The woman turned round, her face concerned. "Should I have? I just knew they were friends. Sera might know." The woman shouted for her daughter who entered the room in a large all-encompassing dress as well. "Do you know the names of Liberty's friends?" asked her mother.

"There's an Anna, that's all I know. Radio person. Otherwise, no. I've never met any of them. Not the person on the beach she meets either."

"Don't be daft, she's walking down there herself. Girls do talk silly sometimes, don't they?"

Hope pondered on this and then watched the girl turn around and ask her mother to fix her dress.

"Wait little one, I'm going to brush my hair."

"I'll get it," said Hope and took up position behind the girl. A glance downwards and then at the back revealed the same style of lace underwear. *Bizarre. Almost like a uniform.* "Do you know where she walked to at the beach?"

"I'll show you," said Sera and ran to the window. Pulling back the curtain, she pointed down to the shore, directly behind the house. "She always went right down there until she went out of sight. She was going down to that part of the beach."

Hope nodded. In her mind she made a note to take a walk down there tonight. "Mrs Carlton, would Liberty by any chance be in contact with Missy?"

The woman turned fiercely and strode right up to Hope's face. "Don't mention anything like that to Papa. She's dead to Papa. Dead. And we don't see her or contact her. Okay? You understand?"

Raising her hands Hope indicated she got the picture. "But

contact exists?" she whispered.

The woman nodded and pulled Hope in closer. "Once a month I see her, in Inverness. Necessary shopping, women's things. Papa won't go near that kind of thing. Otherwise he does the shopping, Papa or Ven sometimes. Missy comes, sees me, sometimes Sera, sometimes Liberty if she's with me."

"Okay, you have a number? I'll be discrete."

The woman looked suspicious but then went to the back of a cupboard. Moving several cardboard boxes and then taking out sanitary pads, she produced a mobile phone. "She rings on this. I don't have her number."

Taking the mobile, Hope switched it on. The device was a simple mobile phone, not one of today's smartphones and it took only a few moments to get into the menu. Hope found the last number that had called in and made a note. "So no one else uses this?"

"No," replied Mama, "and make sure Papa doesn't find out. He won't be happy and I don't want to disappoint him."

"It's our secret. If you are all dressed, we should make our way downstairs and see what my boss wants next. I suspect Papa and Ven will be coming to the station."

"Will they be charged? Papa was only defending us and our home. Please don't make him angry."

"Why? What's he do when he's angry?" Hope saw the younger woman's head droop while Mama kept a stoic face.

"Nothing that he shouldn't," said Mama. "He's got to keep discipline in order to run a house. And he runs it well."

A chill ran up Hope's back. She had the feeling that something was wrong here, gravely wrong, in how the family interacted, but the most frightening thing to her was how Mama stood up for her husband. The mark on the back of the thigh was bothering her as well as the mismatched underwear with the frigid looking outer clothing.

"I need to look at where Sera saw Liberty go. Will you take me Sera, just down to the rear of the house, where you saw her go out of sight?"

"Papa will take you," replied Mama.

"No," said Hope, seeing the younger woman's face light up for a second, "Sera needs to, She knows what she saw and where she saw her sister, so it has to be her. Let's get everyone downstairs and we can get underway before it becomes too cold out there."

Ushering the women downstairs, Hope found Macleod and advised him of her plan. He agreed but insisted on waiting for some backup before she departed. Presently, she retrieved a torch from the car and then set off into the fields at the rear of the house towards the sea.

"What was she wearing?" asked Hope. "The last time you saw her, what was she wearing?"

"Her long green dress. Had a bag with her as well. A large one, like a rucksack," answered Sera who was now smiling and beaming at Hope in the moonlight. Fortunately, the clouds had given way to a bright celestial body that was pouring its faint but welcome light on the area. In fact, at this time there was no need for the torch and Hope saw a pair of white teeth beam from Sera's shadowed face.

"Can I ask you something?"

"Of course," replied Hope, giving the woman a smile.

"What's it like, having a career?"

"A career? Well, it's been good for me, tough at times but good. Why do you ask?"

"Careers are not for women," the girl said in an imitation of her father's voice. "Women are for raising the children."

"Surely that's your choice?" queried Hope.

"Mama said she was happy rearing us, but Missy didn't want that, that's why she's gone. I want to go too. She tells me about her job, and it sounds fun. She works in a bar and people are coming and going, there's music and she gets to dress how she wants when she wants. Like you, she gets to pick out her clothes. You did pick out what you are wearing? I mean, your boss didn't tell you to wear those. He might have done, but the trousers really suit you, especially with the boots. You look great. And I'm rambling, sorry."

"It's fine, ramble away. But listen, no one chooses my clothes. I dress to be practical for my job but otherwise I choose what I wear. DI Macleod is my boss but only in this job. I have freedom to do what I want in my life. And actually DI Macleod's boss is a woman." Hope watched the woman's face become wide-eyed in amazement. "Who picks your clothes?"

The woman began to frown. "Papa. He gives us a selection to choose from, a set for outsiders and a set for when it's just family about. That's what is weird, how you choose for yourself. Mama never would, Papa knows best. It's the way of things, Papa is the head, all papas are."

Hope shook her head as they continued to walk. "Not in this day and age, sister, at least not as much." Looking at the woman, Hope felt angry. "Don't you see any other girls or families? Even television, surely you see how other women live now."

"We don't have a television and Mama schools us. Since Missy did the outside lessons and met the others, Papa makes us stay with Mama. He says they misled Missy, they killed her. But she's okay, I've seen her and she tells me of women like you."

They had trudged to the end of the field and the house was now out of sight. There was a steep slope down and looking to her left in the direction of the bothy, just about visible due to the lights of the forensic team, Hope saw the tide had blocked off the beach.

"Is it always like that or can you get around?"

"You can get past at the right time, I think," said Sera, "but I've never been. Papa doesn't allow it."

Hope made her way down the small slope to the small amount of beach that remained clear of the tide. As she rounded a gorse bush, she saw the faint outline of some material. Reaching down, her hand touched it and it felt coarse, like a handle of a gym bag. Hope pulled and a large bag came out, which she unzipped. There was an array of clothing, skirts, tops, underwear and even a jacket as well as one large dress. Looking back at Sera, Hope noticed she was horrified.

"She can't wear that out here, that's for the house, that's for the family only. Papa will kill her."

# Chapter 9

Macleod watched the marked police car arriving, one more to join the others that had been swift in their response to his call. The night air was cold, and there might be a frost by morning. He thought the forecast had talked about snow but he had not been listening that closely to the radio when he had journeyed up from Glasgow with Hope. A white blanket was not required at the moment and the inherent fun and games that came with driving through slush and ice.

Turning back to the house, Macleod watched his junior as she was talking to the mother. The woman had heard from her daughter about the clothes found at the beach and was now wavering between a quivering wreck and a snivelling fragile pillar for her daughter. Hope was being very tender towards the woman and despite her height, she was able to stoop and make eye contact, no doubt trying to extract more detail.

Shivering in the cold, Macleod watched the red hair of McGrath swish as she talked to the woman and he found himself in this tired moment longing for a private moment. His mind drifted to a warm bed and arms wrapped around him. There were quiet whispers and then a cheeky tickle on his back causing him to jump and flip over looking straight into the face of the woman lying with him. He was glad it was Jane Hislop, the woman who had so recently come into his life. But he was sure the words had come from Hope.

After having been alone for near twenty years, the last case had unlocked the dam of want and hunger he had built over the years and his feelings concerning his professional partner were at best mixed. In reality, they were more like forcibly contained by his common sense and the knowledge it would only work in a fantasy world his mind made up. And anyway, now there was Jane. She was fun, lively, and she seemed interested in him for being him.

"Sir," said Hope walking over to Macleod, bringing him out of his daydream. He tried not to stare as she walked the short distance over to him.

"Anything else?" he asked.

"The clothes are missing from a section of wardrobe that should not leave the house. Apparently the clothes in the bag are for wearing around the house which given their cut seems strange. You'd expect so see them in a nightclub or in summer. They are certainly more sexual, like you're on the pull, trying to bag a man, or woman."

"And yet they are dressed in such frumpy clothes now."

"Because you are here," Hope commented.

"Because the police are here? Seriously, they wear those because the police are here."

"No, sir, because you are here. Males. I don't matter, you see. In fact I think Papa would have me dressed in that sort of gear if you weren't here and he had a choice."

Macleod stopped the image before it came to his mind. "So he's basically a sexist then. He certainly seems to rule the roost. Did you get hold of the other daughter?"

Hope let go a deep sigh and looked away to the sea, the moon shining off it. "Yes, and she'll be on her way up tomorrow to Inverness. I doubt she'll come to the house though and Mrs Carlton doesn't want her husband to know that Missy will be in the vicinity. Worried that the secret arrangement they have will go to the dogs."

"Good that she's coming though, saves us bringing her in and keeps the family dynamic as it was." When he said it, Macleod wondered if he actually meant it. This family life was seriously messed up. "I think we need to go and brief the troops, catch up with Ross. We have our murder victims and hopefully forensics will confirm that."

"Did you catch their names, by the way, I mean their full names?" Macleod shook his head. "The dad is Justin, nothing funny there. The mother is Precious, and then it gets weird. The eldest girl, Missy, is actually Submissive. Her sister is Sera, actually is short for Service, and then comes Liberty, which seems a departure. But the son, Ven, is Vengeance."

Macleod shook his head. "We need to get more detail on the cult or commune or whatever it was they were at in America before they came back. There's a link between our DJ and the missing girl. And there's enough strangeness here to see that Papa might not have been happy that his girl was seeing an older man."

"More like any man," interrupted Hope.

"Well, yes, but there's also enough tension at the radio station. Lot of people to sift through, McGrath. And I need my bed. I'm exhausted. So let's wrap up here and get to this hall where Ross has set up base."

The pair left the family home with different police cars still there, keeping an eye on the family and preparing for any incoming call of the daughter or her arrival, although neither was truly expected. Macleod lay back in the seat as Hope drove and in his mind he could see the smiling face of Jane Hislop. When would he get back to her? It hadn't been a day and yet he felt like a schoolkid on his first crush. *Focus Macleod,* he chastised himself, *there's work to do.*

The car pulled into the small town of Cromarty and Macleod spotted the police cars parked close to a hall beside the football pitch. Once parked, he strolled into the hall, giving his identification to the officer on the door who apologised for doing his job too well. Macleod liked having his ID checked the first time, it showed a diligent trait in the officer. But next time he had better remember. It was no use having an unobservant colleague.

Inside the main hall, he saw a number of tables had been set up with laptops and a crazy run of cables dominated the floor. At the side of the hall a large board had been erected which had photographs of the area of the murders and various maps. Macleod wasn't a great one for diagrams, maps and linking lines, instead preferring to conduct his deductions in his head. But the system helped others come to conclusions and he was aware that it was rarely just his mind that produced a solution to crimes.

Ross beamed at Hope and Macleod nearly swore. Not again, what was it with coming to these parts with her that every man running the room wanted to be with her. Macleod coughed loudly announcing he wanted coffee. Ross hurried off and Hope gave Macleod a stare.

"Bit harsh, sir," she whispered.

"Well, I 'd rather he wasn't checking you out when I arrive."

"I doubt he was doing that."

"No Hope, he blooming well was. I saw him."

"No, sir. He might check you out but not me. I'm not his type. He told me. He does like my boots though."

Macleod didn't respond. He was tired, damn tired and he was not apologising because he could tell between a shoe fetish and rampant male hormones. Carefully, Macleod scanned the room and suddenly thought that the force was getting younger every day. The girl on the far desk for instance, she could have been his daughter. Maybe worse, his grand daughter. *No, she's not that young. And more to the point I'm not that old.*

"Your coffee, sir. I hope it's okay, we didn't have a lot of time so that's just what we had in the store. There's a wee shop here and we'll see what they have tomorrow."

"Okay Ross, it's okay. Just been a long day so let's get on with it. We'll brief the team with where we are at in ten minutes. McGrath will do it. I think that a meeting between our DJ and one of the family is obvious but who knew and was about, that needs tied down."

Ross looked at him quizzically.

"The family, Ross," interrupted Hope, "The Carltons we were just at, where we found the clothing. Looks like their daughter may have been off for a night of romance and wound up getting killed for it."

"Like I said," Macleod continued, "McGrath will brief and then I'm going to get some shut eye and make an early start tomorrow. Have we accommodation in the town? If not I'll lie down somewhere around here."

Macleod left Hope getting her notes in order and walked outside into the cold night. He was simply watching the stars when someone walked past him.

"Aye-aye."

"Hello," said Macleod as the person disappeared along the street, a dog in tow. He heard a second "Aye-aye" to the officer on duty outside the hall. Something was bothering Macleod and had been for the last month. Once again Jane came to mind but it was not Jane that was troubling him. Since the Isle of Lewis case where he had come to terms with his wife's death, he had been at peace about it. But since Jane came on the scene, he had begun to start thinking about his wife again. And in intimate ways. And then he'd start comparing Jane and his deceased wife, whose name was also Hope. He knew it was not healthy but where were these thoughts coming from?

"Sir," said Ross from the doorway, "McGrath's ready when you are."

"Very good, detective, I'll be with you presently." Macleod breathed deeply. Something was not right. He would need to deal with it. But for now, there was a briefing to do.

Macleod stood at the rear of the hall while McGrath ran through the details so far and where investigations would need to continue. There was the cult or commune in America that needed to be investigated. The movements of the family would need to be known. Were there any neighbours? If so, they would need to be interviewed.

Canvassing of the area would also be required, stop and ask techniques as the Black Isle homes were quite spread out. Press statements were discussed and then assembling the movements of those people at the radio station who could have been involved. Forensics would also need to confirm the identity of the bodies. What had come back so far tallied with the thought that Andy MacTavish and Liberty Carlton were the victims and that it was no accident. Petrol had been poured over them, although they were dead beforehand, as the first informant had believed.

The plan for the next day was to get to the radio station and the Carlton house to trace movements around the time of the murders. Also Missy Carlton would need to be interviewed. As the briefing ended, Macleod gave a small speech which he thought was limp and then looked at his watch. Two in the morning, he needed his bed.

Ross handed McGrath a key and directions. Together, Macleod and his partner walked the few streets to their accommodation. The house was dark, and when the lights were turned on, they found two smallish bedrooms, a kitchen, bathroom, cloakroom and a view of the sea where the lights of the Nigg boatyard were burning bright.

"I'll be back in ten minutes," said Macleod, "Just need to stretch my legs." He did not wait for a reply and wrapped himself up tight against the chill and walked to the beach that gave the fantastic view of the yard across the firth.

The tide had retreated somewhat and Macleod made his way onto the beach, stopping by the water. Giving a quick glance around, he then turned, wholly focused on the sea before him.

"It's been too long," he said aloud. "I feel like the first time with us, although this time I probably understand the mechanics. I reckon you'd like her. She's fun, got your sense of humour, always at me to chill out and to be less formal. But the job's half done for her, you did that. Never got to see the results really.

"Do you get to see from where you are? I want to know what you think of Jane, if you approve. Are you happy for me? Or am I still yours? You're still mine, you know that, don't you. This should have been us, should have been our time to have. You should be trying to come to me, finding a place up here while I'm away. Should be your time. I'm sorry I never saw it. I'm sorry I never stopped it. I'm sorry you were alone. I still want you Hope, I still…"

Macleod broke down in tears, his hands covering his face as he wept. His body shuddered from the force of his pain. He fell to his knees, the tide splashing up against him as he wept. And then two hands gently held his shoulders. A glance to the side showed McGrath's boots to be beside him.

"Let it go, Seoras. Let her know, let her know."

# Chapter 10

It felt like four hours of sleep and no more. Macleod stumbled out of his bed, put on a dressing gown and then made for the bathroom where he heard the shower was already on. Deciding to have his breakfast instead, he opened several cupboards in the kitchen, found some cereal, milk in the fridge and coffee in little packets near some mugs. It was not long before he heard the shower end and the occupant climb out and begin to dry herself. Time was precious so he wolfed down his food and prepared to go to the shower himself.

The door to the bathroom squeaked as it opened and Macleod stood up and took his dishes to the sink. As he turned around he found Hope standing in the doorway. Her hair was dripping and a grey towel was wrapped about her body stopping mid thigh where her long legs reminded him of the colour of the milk in the bowl.

"You okay? Did you sleep at all?"

"Yes, I slept," said Macleod. "It's daft, Hope. I have a new woman in my life, and it's going well, but I still feel the need to talk to her. I felt like I was asking permission."

"I'm sure it must be normal, but I can't say. The longest relationship I've had was three months. Apparently I'm hard to live with."

Macleod looked at the white arms and legs, the hair dripping onto the bare shoulders and the slight curl in her smile and wondered how this could be true. She'd been so attentive to him last night as well. Surely any man would be happy with a woman like Hope. And then he realised he was staring.

"I'll get my shower," he said quickly. "The coffee's not great by the way." Macleod watched Hope smirk and then turn on her heel and leave the kitchen. He needed to shower and then make a telephone call to Jane before the day started.

It was twenty minutes later when he heard the ringing tone on the other end of the line and felt the butterflies in his stomach. He was a man of reasonable years, not a teenager on his first love, but there was a trepidation in speaking to *his woman*. Well, she was not quite that yet but it was well on the way. *Wasn't it?*

"Yes," said a bleary voice.

"Sorry it's early, but my day's going to be full and I didn't want to miss speaking to you."

"Hi. How's it going up there? I saw some things on the news. I guess it can't be pleasant dealing with that sort of thing. Have you got very far yet?"

Macleod breathed deeply and tried not to get annoyed. Having told Jane before that he was never going to discuss details of his work with her, she constantly asked. But he could not give her that luxury. Some of the work should only ever be discussed with colleagues. Some of the stuff he saw was not fit for loved ones or families.

"Tell me about your day," said Macleod. "Did you swim?"

"I did," Jane replied, "but there was no one to come into the steam room with me. I had to sit there instead and check out this twenty-year-old guy, six foot four, a chest like a wall and such deep blue eyes. And then, when he swept me up his arms and insisted we make it hot and steamy…"

Macleod laughed. "You were in a steam room, it was already hot and steamy."

"I was on my own, just saying I missed you."

The door to the small lounge burst open and Hope stood there in her jeans and white blouse. "Sorry sir, but it's all kicked off at the Carltons'. Missy's back and there's been trouble."

Macleod nodded at Hope. "Sorry," he said into the phone, "but something's come up. I have to run."

"Okay. Stay safe. I miss you. I really do."

"I'll ring when I can. Sorry, have to run."

With that Macleod stood up and grabbed his coat from the chair before him. He could hear Hope starting up a car already and he grabbed the accommodation keys off the low coffee table. Within a minute, they were driving out of Cromarty in a car collected while he showered.

"Jane alright?" asked Hope.

"Yes. She's good. Was swimming yesterday. Also went in the steam room."

"Well that's good," said Hope, "at least she wasn't out with some other guy. You must mean something to her."

Macleod went to round on her but then saw the smile. He was far too reactive when it came to Jane. But it was also Hope that was causing this. Due to the closeness of their working relationship, how she had helped him when he was falling apart on Lewis and since, they were developing more than a professional attachment. She was becoming a friend, a close one. There were things Hope knew that Jane did not and never would.

Glancing at her figure as she drove the car, he found himself in that male dilemma of mixing up friendship and sexual hunger. Keeping Hope in the confines of mere professional detachment was not easy and in the days before Jane he had allowed his mind to wander to a fantasy he knew would and should never be. It was the tragedy coming back, he had told himself. But even now, when he had a special woman in his life, he found it hard to keep his response to Hope's looks and persona on a level it was meant to occupy. *I really need to see Jane.*

The day was only just beginning with dawn's light breaking through the darkness of night. There was a frost on the ground, but in the distance Macleod saw the thick carpet of heavy cloud moving in their direction. It might have been slow in its arrival but it looked like it held an avalanche of snow ready to drop.

The road to the Carltons' was hard to match to the same route they had taken the night before and Macleod did not recognise any features that had been shrouded by the darkness during their previous journey. In the oncoming daylight, he was able to see the neighbour's house, less than a half mile away with its grazing cows in the fields between. Macleod wondered when uniform would be there, if indeed they hadn't gone in the night.

Turning down the long drive, he saw a new car close to the front door of the house, parked inside of three police cars. Hope parked their own car farthest away and together they approached the house where shouting could be heard. A young officer in uniform on the door nodded at them as they approached and, once he saw their warrant cards, gave a quick precis of what was happening.

"The older sister came back about an hour ago, demanding

to see their mother, but the father got to her first. There was some pushing and shoving and raised voices. The door was shut on our officer briefly and when he got into the room, Missy Carlton had a bloody lip from a probable punch and the father had some marks on his face, like nails dug in. The son was there too but he was not injured. We have a few more officers between them now, but it's still ongoing."

Nodding his thanks, Macleod stepped inside and made for the lounge area where he could hear voices. On opening the door, the room briefly turned to him before getting back to their argument. Papa was on his feet and pointing a finger at a new woman, presumably Missy, while the brother was glowering from one of the large armchairs. Mama was sitting on her knees by Papa's feet, her other daughter beside her. There was a dishevelled look to the family he had seen the previous night, but Papa was in full voice at the new arrival, clearly ignoring the instructions of the officer in the room pleading for calm.

"This is your doing," said Papa, pointing at the new woman. "Running off, taking any man, not knowing your station. I would have found you someone suitable, a real man for you, but you know better. Look at you now, a wee whore, banging your way up the ladder. Letting any man who wants to feast on you. Your place was here, you ungrateful cow. And now you've got your sister killed!"

"I damn well hate you, you sick bastard. You drove her to this, you and your perverted ideas. And look at them, look at what you've done to Sera and Mama. Little dolls, little bloody dolls. I'm glad I got clear of your shit."

Macleod watched the woman race forward and the constable step between father and daughter. But she was quick and slipped under an arm, grabbing the older man. The son rose to his feet as she grappled with her father.

"McGrath!" shouted Macleod as he stepped in front of the son, who pushed out an arm catching Macleod under the chin, driving his head back. Grabbing the son's top Macleod spun and managed to pull the man with him and fell into the warring father and daughter. He tumbled to the floor, the son on top of him and watched Papa and the woman tumble down as well. Across the room in a flash was Hope pulling the new woman to her feet and pushing her back to the other side of the room. Feeling the son try to get up and go for her, Macleod threw his arms around him, preventing him before Macleod was assisted by the constable.

Other officers, presumably alerted by the noise of the fall, ran in and began to make a wall between the parties. Getting to his feet, Macleod pointed at the son. "Sit your backside down in that chair and if you move again without permission I'll take you down the station for everyone's protection." With eyes on fire, the young man reluctantly obeyed.

"Do you want this one outside, sir?" asked Hope, holding the new woman by the arm.

"Yes, I'll be there in a minute. Constable, I want at least two of you in here with the family. They do not leave this room until I come back." Macleod watched the nod of the constable and, satisfied with the serious look on the man's face, he turned to Papa.

"And you will be quiet, sir. There are enough problems at the moment without you adding to them."

"Get that trollop out of here then. And tell her to cover up properly. She was brought up better than that. You hear me, she was—"

"Mr Carlton, I think everyone can hear you. But I don't want to hear you, so kindly calm down, shut up and sit down. Do it or I will take you and your son and lock you in a cell for the protection of everyone else. Am I understood?" Macleod was right in the man's face but he could feel the blood dribbling down his chin and wondered just what sort of image he cut. "I'll be back in here to speak to you presently."

With that Macleod tore out of the room and stepped outside where he breathed deeply. His chin was smarting from the blow he'd received and when he wiped it with his hand he saw the blood. Taking a handkerchief, he dabbed it before looking for Hope and the woman. They were standing by the new car and the woman was lighting a cigarette.

"I presume you're Missy Carlton. Quite an arrival, ma'am," Macleod said as he approached the car. "I'm DI Macleod and this is DC McGrath."

"I'm sorry," apologised the woman. "Where is my sister? Have you any idea? Is it something to do with the bothy?"

"Why do you say that?" asked Hope.

"Well, it's on the news. There's a lot of attention around it. And someone's dead down there, that's what the television says. Is it Lib?"

Macleod studied the woman's face and saw the tears forming behind the eyes. "Why would she be there? What's really happening in this family, Miss Carlton?"

The woman turned her back on Macleod and sucked in another draught of her cigarette. She was wearing black ankle boots, tights or stockings under a skirt that stopped at the knee, with a cream jumper on top that fitted snuggly. In the modern fashion, she did not look like a tart, thought Macleod, but she was showing off what curves she had. He struggled with the contradiction clothing was today. In a world where men were not meant to look, not meant to openly show delight in a woman's appearance anymore, the clothes had seemed to become more body aligned. Everything grabbed any curve that was there to show. Nothing was open to view, but everything was hugged tight to the body.

"My father is a sexist, chauvinist, perverted pig, Detective. During my life I was a doll to be put on show for him and hidden from the outside world. We were all just there to clean, cook and then be on display."

"Prim and neat or was it something darker?" asked Macleod.

Missy laughed and Macleod watched her shake a little preparing her answer. Whether it was the cold or the memory, he could not tell. "Darker, but not that. My father likes his girls to be ready to be a wife. We got the prime example with my mother, always running around in next to nothing for him, tending to his needs."

"That sounds very one-sided," remarked Hope.

"It is. But in his own way he actually cares for her. He sees her as a perfect wife and wanted us all to be like her. I was a bit of a disappointment. I am not someone's lap dog, Detectives, I am independent and quite happy with it. When I left, he struggled to forgive me. But he has."

"Forgive me, Miss Carlton, but that's hard to believe having just seen the two of you go at it in there."

The woman spun around and gazed at Macleod. "He didn't come after me, and he didn't kill me for my disobedience. Given the culture we grew up in, the one they embraced over the pond, I see that as forgiveness."

"But what about the bothy?" asked Hope. "What has the bothy got to do with this family?"

"You found the clothes at the beach, yes?" There was a nod from Hope. "Well, imagine if you will. Your every move is guarded, you have little contact with the outside world, so you need a place to meet them. At first it's a friend, a chum, because you're only eight and that's what you have. You're off to the beach, that's what you tell your Papa, but you make your way round at the correct time, skipping past the tide. It's about having a friend."

Macleod watched the woman shudder and knew this time it was not the cold.

"But when older and more curious, when you have been out in the world a small bit, just for swimming lessons or at a day course for something Mama cannot teach, then it becomes a haven of exploration. It wasn't salubrious, Detectives, but we did what we could. I became a woman in there, as they say, and I taught my sisters about the secret house, the bothy. Lib, used it like me, to meet boys and men she fell for. Not by the hundreds, mind—" Missy laughed "—but there were a few."

"Did you know anyone Liberty was seeing there? We know you were in touch via your mother and that you met your sisters on occasion."

The woman paused before continuing. "Do you see it as sordid? I just wonder what you make of it, our escape, being a father."

Macleod coughed. "I'm not a father. And I'm not here to pass judgement, just to find your sister."

"Of course. Papa found it sordid, even though he pushed us there, keeping us trapped. That was the strange thing I found when I left. I missed him. In his own way, he was quite loving."

"I'm sure he was," said Macleod. "But what about Liberty? Did she tell you anything about the men in her life, anyone who she was engaged with strongly enough to need the bothy?"

Missy flicked the last bit of ash off her cigarette and then threw it on the ground, stamping it out. She then opened her car door and took out another cigarette from a packet on the passenger seat and lit up again.

"She never gave names. There were a few boys at the start, two different ones, but they have been gone over a year and nothing said about them since. Then there was someone close, she said, someone nearby and a man. She kept mentioning his age, being older, and a tattoo she liked on his back, a pair of birds. She was quite taken by him. But recently she said she had a star. She said I would know him, everyone would know him."

"And could you tell?" asked Hope.

"No. How could I? All she said was he was a star. Then kept waffling on about how he was being moved from a different solar system to her system. I didn't follow that bit at all, but then Liberty was more prone to fanciful imagery. Liked her poetry."

Macleod looked at Hope who simply nodded. But he had to be sure. "Miss Carlton, you know we found a bag at the beach down from the house. It had rather engaging clothing in it, nothing explicit but certainly figure hugging and … frisky."

"She's dead then. Our Lib's dead." She drew on the cigarette, her legs now wobbling, and Hope moved forward to support her.

"Why dead? Why do you think she's not simply run away?"

"Because the bag is there for a reason. It's how we worked it. Bag of clothes, change down there into something that made them look. Then get it on in the bothy. And then back before we were missed. She's not back. Your people are all over the place. The news says there's someone dead. Run away? No, Lib's there. Our Lib's there!"

# Chapter 11

Macleod was not delighted about leaving the Carltons together and gave instructions to the sergeant at the house that any out-of-order actions were to be met with a trip to the station. Missy's arrival had given a deeper insight into the family, candid as she was, but Macleod reminded himself that this was her view and like all views would have its own taint. Although he could not blame the girl for leaving for brighter lights.

For some reason today he felt like driving and he gave Hope the task of calling into the forensics department to look for any updates while they travelled over to Inverness to pay a call on the radio station. The road over was pleasant enough and he took the blind corners and winding roads at a sensible speed. There was not the rush of Glasgow here, but it was not the sticks either. Inverness was a booming city, expanding rapidly, and was building a good reputation. But the more people you have the more problems you get, he thought. Still, keeps me in coffee and biscuits.

"Forensics have a positive ID on the male victim," said Hope, hanging up her call. "It's definitely Andy MacTavish, dental records and medical all check out. Still working on the female victim. They are hoping to have her identified by lunch."

"Indeed, no one wants to work over lunch. Ring Ross and let him know what we are up to and tell him I want some progress on the American commune connection, where the Carlton parents got together."

The road to Inverness took the pair through Fortrose and Munlochy and, after having been in Glasgow so long, Macleod found himself enjoying passing through smaller, quieter villages. But soon they were on the main road to Inverness and the Kessock bridge where he found himself briefly delayed due to the large number of cars approaching a roundabout with traffic lights. It seemed the Highlands soon picked up some of Glasgow's traits.

On arrival at the station, Macleod clocked the receptionist staring at them out of the large glass window and he thought he saw some nervousness. It was not usual to be greeted in this fashion, even if the person in question had committed no crime, but he believed this girl was hiding more than she had told Hope. The rough-cut Romeo that MacTavish was turning out to be may have set up a line of jealous women and maybe one had been handy with a weapon or even with their fists. He imagined Hope could soon bludgeon someone if she really wanted to.

"You see if you can find this other DJ, Mochilas, see if anything is happening from that front. I want to put a wee bit of pressure on Anna Campbell. She might have been jealous of her friend; after all, people do a lot worse to those they think they love."

"She seemed genuine to me," said Hope.

"Yes Detective, but best to get the male perspective too and then cross reference." Looking at Hope, Macleod saw a questioning stare and he realised he had walked into the whole battle of the sexes argument again. "Look, I'm not saying you're not right, but sometimes we read things differently, men and women, and its sometimes worth a check on each other. If I thought you couldn't read people you wouldn't be here, Hope. It's just we have different angles, different perspectives. I might just see or happen upon something you might not." Hope did not look convinced. "And vice versa of course."

"Of course, sir."

With a deliberate shrug of the shoulders, Hope marched off in front of Macleod and he let out a sigh. I can't win, I just can't win when it comes to this damn man-woman thing. Watching her disappear into the studio building, Macleod was reminded what a figure Hope cut. Damn brave man though to take her on. She'd keep you on your toes but she'd be surely worth it. Probably best just being her boss, he chortled inwardly.

The foyer of the radio station was warm and Macleod suddenly felt his overcoat was too much and started to shed it. Whilst Hope had disappeared past reception into a corridor on the left, Anna Campbell was on the telephone but she still approached from behind her desk, all the while talking into her headset. Without a word, she took his coat and placed it on a hanger and then onto a rail inside a large cupboard.

While she was still talking, Macleod looked around at the pictures on the walls noticing Anna in several of them. However, as the years became more recent she seemed to disappear. He looked more closely and saw Anna in the two years previous to the last two as being a permanent feature on the award pictures. Then she was absent. Andy MacTavish was suddenly flanked not by staff but by his wife.

"Detective, I am sorry for that, can I help you? Mrs Tulloch is in a meeting but I can see if I can interrupt if you wish."

"Actually, Miss Campbell, I wanted to talk to you. But first a wee question from something I've just noticed. These award pictures, Mr MacTavish seemed to do rather well."

The woman snorted. "Don't trust those," she said. "Awards mean nothing, ratings are what counts, ask my boss."

"But you attended them?"

"Of course, why not? It's a night out."

"But what happened? Did you fall out of favour?" Macleod stared hard, trying to unnerve the girl.

"His actions with younger women sort of came to the fore and his wife insisted on her being beside him."

"Seems reasonable," Macleod said, pitching a ball up to see if it would be struck.

"That cow. She doesn't know shit about her husband or what makes him tick. If she was looking after him then maybe he wouldn't have wandered."

It struck Macleod that if he had made that remark it would have been deeply sexist but because it was said by the adulterous woman then it was fair comment. Again, he could not work out this whole man-woman thing.

"But you didn't satisfy him either," pitched Macleod, "after all, there have been others since you. Your friend for instance."

"You're not like your colleague. She was nice, understood my concern for my friend. I would never have touched Lib, she was put upon enough by her father already. She needed some time out in the sun, and Andy gave her that. I was happy for her."

"But angry at him?" The question hung in the air and Macleod knew he had hit the button. "Where were you two nights ago?"

"Home, in my flat once work was done."

"And when were you at work the following morning?"

"I was here for nine, ask anyone."

There was time then, thought Macleod, definitely time.

"But you need to look at that family. They did it to Lib, they did everything to that girl."

"I'll look at them," said Macleod, "but which car is yours?"

"The red hatchback, beside the green coupe." The words were mumbled and Macleod saw the worry on her face.

"Thank you," he said and he saw the relief sweep across her face. "We'll speak again." The worried look came back.

Macleod indicated that he wanted to speak to Anna's boss now and the girl scuttled down the corridor to the office of the station manager. Whilst he waited, Macleod decided to have a wander in the other direction and passed through a set of double doors that Hope had disappeared through. He stood in a corridor with a number of rooms on either side, little windows set into each. Through the first one, he could see Hope talking to a DJ but with all the lights and switches in the studio apparently live and a number of people in the room beside it. On the other side of the corridor was another studio with a woman sitting alone in a chair rustling through paperwork and tapping into a computer every now and then.

"Our studios, Inspector. Jimmy is being very helpful, I see. He's actually on air and must be answering questions between sections. That's really above and beyond."

Macleod turned around and looked at Laura Tulloch standing in her high heels and black skirt. The tight-fitting blouse, the length of her skirt, somewhat shorter than yesterday, and the subtle but masterfully applied make-up gave her an engaging look and whilst Macleod appreciated it, he understood what it meant. She knew he was coming after last night's shenanigans at the MacTavishes' and she was ready to charm.

"What is above and beyond is my detective not hauling him out to the station for questions or insisting he leave the show. I have a murder inquiry, frankly everything else needs to stop, not the inquiry."

"So you've confirmed it's Andy."

"I never said that. I guess his death would be a good solution to an awkward problem."

Laura Tulloch looked shocked before composing herself. "I'd never stoop to that. We have other ways to move workers on, Detective."

"But none seemed to be working."

"Walk with me to my office, please. I really don't want to speak candidly out here in the open."

Macleod nodded and followed the woman through the double doors, back down the corridor to her office. Inside, she offered him a seat and then asked if he cared for a drink.

"I don't," said Macleod.

"On duty."

"I don't on or off. Devil's brew they called it when I was growing up and I've seen it do too much damage. But as I was saying, his death would be a boon to you."

"Really," said Laura, "that's uncalled for."

"Is it? His wife wasn't too keen on you last night."

Macleod watched the woman pour a large tumbler of whisky and waited for her to add water and ice. She didn't, and then she dropped the contents down her throat in one go. Carefully, she set the tumbler down and walked to a chair beside Macleod, perching elegantly on the end of it, her bare legs showing.

"She accused me of bringing him down, has-been that he

was. Sorry, is. Don't get me wrong, Detective, if he's gone then my life here will be easier, but we don't do that. And if I have to put up with that cow calling me once more I will flip. She accused me of actually having an affair with her husband and dropping him. Said I tried to sleep him out of the contract. Really, I think he's somewhat beneath me. I don't sleep with my workers. I prefer stronger men than that."

Macleod noted the look and the tilt forward toward him. Her hand reached forward and touched his leg. Looking up, he watched her smile, run her tongue slowly around the edge of her lips before standing and pouring herself another drink. She was certainly intoxicating for her age, but she had picked the wrong man in Macleod.

"I'll be frank," he started, "I don't think you slept with him because basically you are too old for his tastes. Don't gave me that hurt look, you are over twenty-five so I doubt you would have appealed. You are a bit classier than that. You would have pushed and extorted to whatever degree kept you just legal, but it would be too risky in your position to go further. There are always other jobs. But be warned, something's wrong in this radio station and I will find out what. As for you, don't be so forward and don't flirt at a man like me in that way. You really are quite beautiful, but when you go on the attack like that, it's just unappealing."

With that he stood and heard the words "Cheeky bastard" uttered behind him. Smiling, he opened the door and saw Anna Campbell hurrying down the corridor. Now you, Miss Campbell, you are hiding something.

# Chapter 12

Sometimes, the boss is still a dinosaur, thought Hope. Ignoring Anna Campbell, she turned into the corridor away from the offices and found the studios laid out on either side of the passage. On one side she saw a man in his thirties, broadcasting away, the red light of the studio telling her he was live. On the other side a woman seemed to be preparing, a keyboard and a heap of notes in front of her. She was looking consistently at a screen, nodding her approval when she typed something.

Hope saw the red light go out in the studio and simply opened the door.

"Hi, hope you don't mind but I need to ask you some questions."

"Actually, love, if you don't mind I'm in the middle of a show." The man seemed quite put out. "And who the hell are you anyway?"

"Detective Hope McGrath and I need to ask you some questions. You can either get someone to cover or you can just talk to me during the records. I have no problem doing this down the station if needs be, but I didn't want to cock up your day. Sit here, do I?"

The man glowered at Hope before pulling out a chair. She

smiled back and sat in her seat and looked around. She nearly jumped when the man began speaking in a cloy, happy-to-be-here style, which Hope decided she never wanted to wake up to. As soon as he began, he stopped and the red light that had quickly burned went out again.

"Okay, what do you want? Can you make it quick? I'm doing the show."

In the window opposite, Hope could see arms waving at her and fingers pointing so she drew out her warrant card and badge, holding it clearly up to the onlookers.

"Should keep them off our backs," said Hope. "Now then, I see you got what you always wanted. How is it, sat in the big chair?"

"That's uncalled for."

"Is it? We got the impression from your station manager that you were gagging to get in here. Not a big fan of Mr MacTavish either, I hear."

"Look," said the man, running a hand through his healthy but sleek hair, "I'll make no bones about it, it's a good job he's gone. He was bringing the station down, we were in free fall ratings wise. And all because of his stupid contract."

"Yes, kind of hard to shift. Would take something dramatic to get rid of him."

"Stop that. No one would do that."

"Someone did," said Hope, "and they took someone else with him."

"Probably some slut, amazed it's not Anna Campbell, she was all over him, the wee tart. He's best gone. Surprised you didn't grab him for child abduction the age of the girls he was with."

"The younger men not enough for them?" quipped Hope.

Jimmy "The Gen" Mochilas was about to retaliate when the red light came on and he momentarily huffed and puffed before a mass of waving hands in the window opposite brought him back to his show and he blurted out the name of a track. Laughing inside, Hope admired how good she was at getting men's backs up. When the music came on, she smiled at him, awaiting his comeback now the red light had extinguished.

But he was calm. "So he's dead then. Really?"

"We're just about to announce it."

"At the bothy?"

"I never said that. But it is true. Where were you the night before last? Do you know who Andy was seeing?"

"I'm sure he was seeing some new girl. He had boasted about some new bit of skank." Skank, thought Hope, this guy was an oldie. "Apparently she was hot on him. A looker, too, he had said in the car park the week previous. Anna Campbell was beside him and gave him a look like death for that comment. I'm just surprised the sex didn't kill him, an OAP like he was."

"He was forty," interjected Hope, "hardly past it. And this girl seemed to like him then. Where was she from?"

"Black Isle, he said. She hadn't had that much action before, was good in the sack though. Very complicit, went along with anything he wanted."

Hope was beginning to think Andy MacTavish's demise was not at all a bad thing. But she didn't get to judge, just find out the who, where and whys of it all.

"Have you ever been to that bothy?"

"No. Never."

"How do you know? Can you tell me where it is exactly?"

"Well no, but I haven't been to any round there. I'm never on the Black Isle, I don't know anyone there."

"And again, two nights ago, where were you?"

And the red light came on, but Hope held her stare watching The Gen looking back at her as he spoke, announcing the travel and news. She watched him write as he spoke and then he pushed the pad towards her. "Home alone." That's convenient, thought Hope, very convenient.

She heard a noise outside and watched Anna Campbell's rear exit the corridor and then caught Jimmy looking after her. The red light extinguished.

"Have you ever got it on with Anna?" Hope watched the man swallow hard and then shake his head. "Ever asked?"

"She likes the elderly, what can I say? Weirdo of the highest order."

"Or maybe a woman of taste?"

Jimmy raised his eyebrows at Hope and she felt it was all with just a touch too much effort. The guy's previous look said he was into Anna Campbell and was somewhat annoyed not to have been there. What is it with this place? Does working radio make you horny?

After a small slot where Jimmy spoke to a caller, the music came on again. He sat back awaiting the next question and Hope decided to be quiet. Then, just as he was about to sit back up and prepare for his next section, Hope quickly fired in a question.

"So, which car is yours?"

"Don't drive!"

"Why?"

"Not allowed, too many points."

"Drink?" Hope asked as the red light came on. There was a silence that seemed to annoy the people through the glass who waved at Jimmy, imploring that he speak. But he sat there staring with angry eyes at Hope. Then some music kicked in and the voice of the studio manager came over demanding Jimmy snap into action.

Hope felt her mobile vibrate in her pocket and took it out, staring at the message before her.

Jimmy Mochilas traced to using a taxi two nights ago, 1:00 a.m., destination—the Black Isle, approximately one mile from the bothy, Ross.

Staring at the DJ, she watched him blabber on about some single in the charts and then crack a pretty lame joke; Hope smiled inwardly. The DJ finished off with a flourish and then rounded on Hope as the red light went out again.

"So then, are you finished with me?"

Hope held the message on her mobile up to the man's face and watched his expression change from confidence to panic in an instant. "I think you need to get someone to cover for a bit, don't you?"

"It's not what you think it is," he said in a panic.

"It looks like you lied to me."

"No, well, yes, but not because I did anything I shouldn't have. Well, that's not true, but it wasn't a murder. It was a woman I was seeing. She's been thinking her husband has been playing around and she came on to me in a bar and asked if I wanted a little fun so she could get revenge. And then she rang me and it was all very real. Sorry, but it's near the bothy, that's why I didn't want to say. I knew you'd put two and two together and get ten. I was only seeing a woman, that was all."

"Name, address and you will not leave here until we come back for you. In fact, I'm bringing uniform to stay here until I corroborate your story." Hope stood up and stared at the now petrified man.

"I don't know her real name, she called herself Scarlett, but she was blonde. Thought she looked like an actress. She doesn't, even out of her clothes. Actually, she wasn't much cop at all. Pretty disappointing."

What an arrogant prick! I should deliver his balls to her husband. "I'll be right here until uniform arrive. You ring no one and no one else speaks to you. Address?"

"I don't know."

Bringing up the mapping system on her mobile Hope showed the screen to the DJ. "Show me." She watched as he moved in narrowing down the location. She looked at the screen. Bloody hell, she thought, that's the house next to the Carltons'. "You'll be going down the station after this show to make a statement, but you can stay here while I corroborate your story."

"Don't tell her husband. Promise me you won't tell her husband, he's a butcher, he's a bloody butcher."

Hope stood up with her serious face focused on the DJ. Then she turned her back and her face erupted into a mess of silent laughter. Bloody butcher, priceless, just priceless.

# Chapter 13

"Anna Campbell's definitely involved in this." Macleod gave an assured nod as Hope looked at him with questioning eyes.

"Seems a bit much she gave up her friend if she was involved."

"It's standard though, isn't it, nowadays, people messing about, no single partners, all chopping and changing, taking on women and men half their age." He gave a "Humph" and Hope took exception.

"So in older days there was no messing about? That's not what I heard. Plenty of people at it. The sixties was a banging fest!"

Banging fest? She's so crude at times. "I admit that in older days this kind of thing happened, but at least in those days, Hope, we knew it was wrong. Today it's just a lifestyle choice to sleep around." His phone beeped. "Ah, the people living next door to the Carltons are the Tunnocks. Let's see if she's a sassy film star, Scarlett Tunnock."

"I doubt that's her real name," replied Hope.

"Of course it isn't. Provocative name though."

"Really?"

"Yes, Gone with the Wind and all that."

"Haven't seen it."

Macleod tutted. Whilst saying the Tunnocks were neighbours to the Carltons, there were still about five hundred metres between the houses. The driveway down to the house from the main road was well paved and had small lights at the side. There was an elegantly decorated tree at the entrance too. As they pulled up, Macleod saw the rather expensive sports car and the practical but still pricey estate car.

Hope approached the door and rang the bell. They stood between pillars and looked into a pristine hallway. After a few moments, a woman in high heels and a tight skirt appeared. She opened the door and greeted them before looking a little bemused when they pulled their warrant cards out.

"But you people have been here already, they asked us questions. We haven't seen anything."

"It's just routine, ma'am," said Macleod. "You are the closest neighbours. Is your husband in too?"

"Why yes, he is. If you'll come through, Detective. Such a young girl with you as well." The woman led the way and took the detectives along her hall, through the kitchen area and then out into a covered extension, which housed a swimming pool. "This is Detective Inspector Macleod and his young assistant. This is my husband Jim Tunnock and I'm Alison."

Macleod chortled inside at the young assistant comment but failed to catch Hope's eye. He watched Mrs Tunnock sit down and then addressed Mr Tunnock.

"Good day, sir. Sorry to disturb you, but as you are the neighbours to the Carltons who are having some difficulty, I would like to run over any observations you may have made. How do you find them as neighbours? Strange, quiet or what?"

Jim Tunnock was a tall, six-foot man with brown hair and shoulders that could lift mountains. Unlike his wife, who was petite and shapely, Jim looked like he did what was said on the tin. "Never had much bother from them, can hear the odd argument but nothing I would call over the top. They are a bit strange though. Don't really talk to you. And…"

"What sir?" asked Macleod.

"Well, in the summer they often have barbecues and the like out their back but it's a bit weird."

"In what way."

"They are all, well actually no, the women are kind of on show. Not wearing much. How do I put it delicately with women present?"

"You never put it delicately when you were gawking at them," Alison Tunnock cut in. "He was staring at them through the telescope upstairs. Taking it all in, girls and the mum wearing just about zip. I entered the room and he thought I was his mate. 'Look at the baps on that,' he said. To me! His wife! Can you believe it, Detective?"

"That's not really why I'm here, Mrs Tunnock, and while I regret your husband looks at other women and feels the need to talk about it, I'm more concerned with the behaviour demonstrated by the Carltons. Are the men dressed in a skimpy fashion?"

"No," replied Alison. "Typical of my luck. The husband's not much but their young lad's quite the stud."

What's in the water up here? thought Macleod. "Two nights ago, did you see anything strange around here?"

"Well, you'd better ask Alison, she was out and about, I was sat here in the house."

Blushing a little, Alison replied, "Getting some hot flushes and that, time of life I guess. I like to take a walk at night to cool down."

"You were three hours, woman. Where did you go?"

Alison went red. "It's your fault, I know you had a girl here. Admit it, you've been seeing a girl for a while. Was it one of them over the fence? Did you see her? Was it the young one? Nice and handy for you?"

"Don't you dare. You were off and getting some, letting whatever young fool would have you."

"Whoa," shouted Hope. "Just hold it. This is important. You might have cheated on each other, have marriage issues or whatever, but we need to know certain things, namely were you two with anyone two nights ago? I ask because we have a dead girl and we need to exclude you from a murder enquiry. Your infidelity, marriage issues and whatever else is, frankly, sad but not our concern. So one at a time. Mrs Tunnock, were you with someone?"

The woman sat down on a pouffe cushion and held her head in her hands. "Yes, that prick from the radio station."

"Which one?" Macleod interjected quickly.

"Said he was getting the breakfast show, made out he was a big star. I didn't care. I just wanted to teach my bastard of a husband a lesson."

"A lesson. A lesson for what?"

"For screwing any pretty thing that comes your way. I know about them all. It was bad enough seeing you look, but you kept a scorecard. Seriously, you shit. You kept a scorecard. And I wasn't even a five out of ten."

Oh heck, thought Macleod. We don't need this. This is going to get bitchy and angry rather than getting to the point of what happened beyond their flings. "Okay, Mrs Tunnock, let's stick to the where and whens, not so much of the whys yet. "What time were you with him?"

"Until about three. Then he had to run. Saying that the last hour was awkward as he had finished somewhat early. Even more disappointing than you, Jim." The woman rose and laid a punch on her husband.

"Hey, enough," said Macleod. "Does that tally, Mr Tunnock? When did you see your wife?"

"Yeah it does," he said reluctantly, shaking his head.

"And that was when his floosy left. He must have seen me coming because she did a runner and drove off in her red car."

"So your adulterous partner left you about three in the morning, Mr Tunnock?"

"My adulter ... Yeah, she did."

"And her name?"

"Anna, that's all I know. Called herself Anna when we met downtown the previous night. Offered it on a plate when she saw me looking. You don't refuse something like that, Detective. Been a while since Alison had a rack like that."

Smarting, Alison Tunnock took a swing and clocked her husband square on the jaw. She yelled and cradled her fist as he simply sat there. "You callous prick. I hope you catch something from her. And I bet she's got something to do with all this nonsense at the bothy. You're in it up to your neck."

With that Alison stormed out of the room and Hope made to follow. Jim Tunnock grabbed her by the arm. "Is she right?" he asked, his face a little desperate.

About her description of you, highly possible. As for the case I couldn't comment." Hope walked off following Mrs Tunnock.

"Sit!" barked Macleod as the man went to stand. "I'm far from finished."

The man looked stunned but sat back in his seat. "Do I need

a lawyer?"

"You tell me," said Macleod. "Now, you and Anna Campbell were here two nights ago and then your wife walked in on you. I need to know what you did after your wife came in and where Anna Campbell went."

"Why not ask Anna? You obviously know her. She was just a cheap fling for me, a bit of skirt. Young ones are so frisky, don't you find? Right filly you have there."

Macleod stepped forward until he filled the man's complete vision. "Listen and listen good. One, I don't chase skirt. Two, you call my officer a filly again I'll haul you up for abusing an officer. Tell me," he said, clearly angry, "did Anna have any connection to the Carltons that you knew of?"

"Well, she did mention one of them, I can't remember which one it is, I mean I can't remember her name. Cute ass, really cute ass, looked great out their back. Anna and her had met and been out on occasion. Anna's a bit of a girl really. Been around for her age too, likes the older man. You would have a good chance."

Macleod ignored the jibe and instead turned to the window, slowly walking around the swimming pool. "Did Anna ever ask you to do anything for her? I mean you were obviously the rebound figure. Just a bit on the side to keep her going."

"Hey, I'm no one's extra bit of stuff. I'm the real deal."

"Not to Anna. Andy Howlin' MacTavish is who she really wanted. Spurned her as well. Just wondered if she wanted you to give her a hand in a bit of revenge in exchange for jiggling her bits in front of you. You look like someone who could be paid off in that fashion." Macleod saw the man squirm. It was a shot in the dark question, but he saw that the line had just jerked and he needed to land his fish.

"We didn't do anything. But she told me that MacTavish was going to the bothy with the girl from next door. She knew that and she wanted me to come with her to look. Said she was scared of the dark or some bollocks like that, but I said no, especially after Alison had come back. I don't mind doing it al fresco but it was damn freezing. Might have dropped off it was that cold."

It was difficult to know which was more shocking, the easy way this man spoke about an affair or the way in which he commented about his manhood dropping off when he was possibly involved with a murderer. The man was clearly driven by what was between his legs, but he was a good link into Anna Campbell's actions.

"So, Mr Tunnock, you are saying you didn't see Anna after she left?" The man nodded. "Did you see inside her car at any point? I mean that night, not generally."

"Yeah I did, when she arrived, but why do you want to—bloody hell!"

"What? What is it?"

"She had a set of knives on the front seat. I nearly sat on them. I opened the door when she arrived and jumped in to take a hold of her and the corner caught my backside. She said it was for her kitchen, her others had broken or some bollocks like that. Shit, did she…?"

"Excuse me," said Macleod and pulled out his mobile phone. "Ross? It's Macleod. Get Anna Campbell into custody, suspicion of murder. And how far did we search the site around the bothy? Okay, we need to make that go back to the road and up that hill behind. No. Not just the path but the whole hillside. Looking for a knife or maybe two. Soon as sun is up. But we need Campbell now. And get me a squad car over to the Tunnocks' … yeah the Carlton neighbours. They need taking in for some statements."

Macleod turned away from Mr Tunnock and looked out of the window. I knew she was involved, I damn well knew it. As he smiled to himself, he heard Hope walk into the room and turned around to face her.

"Sir, we need to lift Jimmy. Alison Tunnock said he dropped her off close to here but then he stayed in the area. She was going to go out and see why he was still here but her husband being around meant she never got the chance."

"I just told them to pull in Anna Campbell. She had knives in her car when she was with Mr Tunnock. I've ordered a search through the undergrowth and surrounding area tomorrow morning."

The mobile rang again. "Macleod! What's up, Ross? Her car? What do you mean? That's at the crime scene. But was there no one there? Okay, so she came from a distance. I'm on my way, get the squad car to the Tunnocks' and take them in for questioning."

Macleod closed his mobile and saw Hope waiting expectantly. "It's Anna Campbell. Ross was giving out the order to find her and one of the squad cars spotted her car near the crime scene. No one in it. Some sandwiches though, uneaten, on the passenger seat. But she's missing. Time to take a look, McGrath, I think we might be on to our killer. I told you she was up to something."

# Chapter 14

Hope spun the wheel and the car raced round the tight corner. Macleod felt the back wheels slip, but he remained calm as his partner flung the vehicle along the road as fast as she could. Inside he felt the adrenalin pumping and the concern growing for Anna Campbell. What was her car doing here? Abandoned during the day, why?

As they pulled up to a point on the road some three hundred meters from the greenery that led to the bothy and the overgrown slope above it, Hope threw off her belt and exited the car quickly. The concern was evident on her face and Macleod knew she had formed some sort of personal connection to Anna. It happened in cases. Macleod's opinion of the girl was more detached and he was unsure of her exact involvement but he had a feeling it would not be good.

"Any ideas where she could have gone?" Hope asked the constable standing beside the car.

"Well, there's the track down to the bothy back there but we have had someone there and forensics have been back briefly this morning so that's not really an option. We would have seen her."

"Anywhere else near here?" asked Macleod.

"Inland is just farms but you can get to the beach and various coves if you walk that way to the slopes. But it's steep and there aren't any real paths, certainly nothing obvious. But it's a possibility."

Macleod stood and pondered while Hope studied the grass around the car. Why park here? What else is around here? No one would have decided to meet at the bothy; they would have suspected we would still be here. So where?

Watching Hope, he saw her walk over to the undergrowth that started close to the road. There were trees beyond. She turned this way and that, growing more frustrated. Then she suddenly tore into the hedge before jumping over a wire fence. Macleod stood his ground, deciding not to risk the gorse. Within a minute Hope had returned holding the remnants of a sandwich.

"What's the filling in her sandwich?"

Macleod opened the car and grabbed the packet. "Chicken and sweetcorn."

"Bingo, sir. This way."

Macleod followed his partner through the prickly hedge, struggled over the wire fence and found himself on what he would have termed a sheep's path. A very narrow track, made through continued wearing, led into the trees and he followed Hope as she tore along it. Struggling to keep up with her pace, he puffed as they reached a proper line of trees with no leaves but branches remaining at head height. High above, the greenery was evident, but below, where there was little sunlight, everything was brown bark, tree debris, loose needles and soil beneath their feet.

"Over here," said Hope. "There's a disturbance in the soil, like someone sliding down the hillside. You can hear the sea below. I reckon it heads down to the beach. The tracks are pretty fresh."

Macleod felt the cold nipping at him, and out of the sunlight it felt ten times worse than even his late-night walk in Cromarty. Before him Hope slid down the slope, churning up the soil, but he found his feet sticking until he eventually tumbled forward and started falling down what was a steep slope. He hit a tree with his shoulder and then barrelled into Hope's feet taking her down on top of him.

He felt a hand grabbing his. "Come on, Seoras. She might still be down here."

His lungs were gone but he hauled himself up and fumbled his way behind Hope. Focusing on his feet he didn't see her halt before him and clattered into her back. But she was unmoved and she grabbed his arm pointing to a gap in the trees.

"Look, sir, another little house, another bothy perhaps. There's a fire inside too. Come on."

And she was away again. Macleod drove his feet on and found himself following Hope through another bush and onto a better sheep's path, which started to run alongside the hill in the direction of this new house. Hope was now outrunning him by a distance and he lost sight of her. But there was a smell in the air, a burning smell, possibly from the house they had seen. There was petrol in the scent but also something else. He recognised it and his mind flashed back to the bothy they had visited a few days ago and then to a Glasgow warehouse earlier in his career. You never forgot the smell of burning human flesh.

With a greater urgency he drove his feet on and tried to ignore the demand his body was making for more oxygen in a faster flow. The path broke the cover of the trees and the house was before him. The path was arriving at the rear of the building and he could hear the sea possibly only a few metres on the far side of the house. From the size of it, there would be very few rooms on one floor and he was surprised to find no door on the side, simply a gap.

Entering, he saw Hope lying on the floor, her head bleeding as she lay prostrate, her front to the ground. His head screamed intruder somewhere but he was too slow and then felt something solid hit him in the ribs. Turning, he grabbed hold of a coat and tried to find purchase with his feet, but his assailant hit him with a punch to the head.

Macleod fell to the floor but had the presence of mind to roll and avoided a foot coming at his head. Desperately, he tried to get up but was grabbed as he stood and pushed across the room. He saw before him a small fire and flung his hands out, stopping himself from going into it, but his face was inches from a burning mess. The heat seared his cheeks and he felt his attacker grab his shoulders trying to push him in.

Macleod pushed as hard as he could, trying to keep his face from being driven into the fire. The cloying fumes smelled of human, and the heat was causing him pain, but his desperate strength was holding for now. Gradually he felt himself beginning to succumb. Without waiting any longer he let his arms go. One went forward and landed in the fire, supporting him. The other swept back and found his attacker's jaw. He squeezed hard, yielding a cry. He then punched hard backwards before pushing himself away from the fire.

Again he reached for the assailant who was on the floor but only grabbed the coat. Something fell out and Macleod grabbed it. The small plastic device was covered by his hand like it was priceless. A kick to his head caused Macleod to yelp and he tried to roll away again. But he was picked up onto his feet and thrown head first into a wall. The world rang out in his ears, he felt pain surround him and then slumped to the floor. He heard his attacker running away but couldn't turn around to see them. Instead he lay on the ground rolling in pain.

"Hope! Hope! Dammit Hope, answer!"

Macleod rolled over to her and pushed her red hair away from her face. Her eyes were closed but he noted her nostrils flaring. Thank you, God, thank you! He pushed her back, moving her arm under her head into what he thought was loosely the recovery position, but she was not stirring. Getting slowly to his feet, Macleod felt the burn on his hand and looked at it. The skin was red and he fought the urge to cover it in something. It was so hot, the pain shooting up his arm. He looked around and grabbed his mobile from his pocket. He vaguely remembered grabbing the assailant's mobile as well and scanned the floor for it, locating it beside a wall. Checking both mobiles Macleod found there to be no signal. He pocketed both and turned to a motionless Hope.

"I'll be back real soon. Just don't leave. You're one of the best things in my life at the moment, girl, so damn well don't leave."

Staggering out of the small house, Macleod felt his hand raging. He looked for a stream but then heard the sea on the other side of the house. He jumped down a small slope and ran across rocks to the tide and placed his hand in the cool sand as the salt water ran over it. He screamed in pain. He must have had a cut somewhere, but he ignored the pain, choosing to get the cool of the water instead.

After a few minutes, he lifted himself back up and ran back across the rocks, climbing up the slope and finding the sheep's path they had come along. He pushed himself with all he had before finding the slope back up, the churned up ground making the route obvious. Macleod had no idea how long it took before he found the wire fence and gorse bush. Placing one foot on, he swung the other up, but his balance was unsure and he fell over the fence into the gorse and had to roll clear, his face taking a serious scratching in the process.

He looked along the road from his position on the ground. There was the squad car still there but no one inside. Opening the door, he grabbed the airwave radio he found inside. It took a few moments but he managed to relay a message to the control centre. They advised that two officers had gone after him in support but they must have taken a different track. Reinforcements were on the way.

He lay back in the seat, the pain becoming stranger as the adrenalin wore off. Then he started to wonder what had just happened. But the next thing was a tap at the window and a medic was attending him, taking care of his hand and his severely bruised head.

"Hope? How's Hope?" he yelled into the face of the medic.

"Calm down, just calm down," came the reply . The medic shouted over to someone, but Macleod closed his eyes again as the pain was strong. When he opened them, he saw Ross standing there.

"We are getting her to the hospital, sir. She's okay, awake now, but she was out for a while it seems. The lifeboat are taking her in, just a lot easier access for them. And you are on the way there too in a moment.

"No," said Macleod. "There's a body in the fire down there. Get forensics, I think it's Anna Campbell. Find out where everyone is, the Carltons, the Tunnocks, everyone at the station. They couldn't get back too quickly. We need to move on this so we can find the killer."

Ross nodded and ran off to his car. Well, thought Macleod, whoever threw me about had strength. Difficult to be sure it was a man but felt like it. Tunnock could have gone for Anna, but that would be crass and obvious. Maybe the DJ, Hope said he was annoyed with her. The station head? The Carltons? Who knows how many people they hate or how they see folks. It's so open.

Ross returned and asked if Macleod would like to go with him to the Carltons'. Macleod didn't wait and removed his hand from the medic who simply stared at him. The wheels of the car spun in the snow and within minutes they were at the Carltons'. There was an officer stationed outside the front door and as Macleod made his way to open it, the officer stepped across and advised that the parents were having some private time upstairs and he was sure a knock on the door would be best. Macleod ignored him and threw the door open. He tore into the living room and saw Sera sitting in a short dressing gown and underwear. Shaking his head he walked through to the kitchen but saw no one. Opening another door downstairs, he found Missy, dressed in jeans and a tight top listening to her mobile, headphones as large as anything on her head. Next he tore upstairs where Papa came falling out of a door hauling his trousers up.

"What the hell's this?" the man asked.

"Where's your wife?"

"In the room, we've just been doing the things a man and his wife should do alone." But his last words were unheard as Macleod opened the door and saw Mama on the bed, the duvet pulled up to her chin.

"Apologies," said Macleod and tore into the nearby rooms. Each yielded nothing and he returned downstairs to the lounge. On opening the door, he saw the son of the family sitting in the chair Macleod had been told was the son's when he was there previously.

"Where have you been?"

"On the toilet."

Macleod shook his head. Blast, wrong house. "Quick, Ross, the Tunnocks'." With that Macleod turned on his heel and exited the house. Behind him, he heard Papa yelling about decency and privacy. And your girl is sitting there in next to nothing, hypocrite!

# Chapter 15

Macleod stood outside of the Tunnocks', flat, empty and tired. They had raced there, Ross and him, but they had found both of the Tunnocks at home and claiming they had been there all day. Sure, they had not seen each other, but they were each sure they had heard the other. None of the cars had gone missing and Alison Tunnock had been painting in the lounge. The work detailed could have taken her most of the day as far as Macleod could ascertain and Jim Tunnock had been in his garage, working on an old car. They had seen each other several times. An alibi but not a watertight one.

Forensics were now making their way to the house where Anna Campbell's body lay. At least he thought it was Anna Campbell, there was no reason to doubt it. It had been her following the path from her car, she couldn't be contacted now and anyone who knew her could not find her. But who was his assailant?

Ross was to take him to the pier at Avoch where he would board a boat that would take him to the house by the rocky beach. Not just him but more experts and equipment for forensics. It was the easiest way down apparently, not that Macleod minded being on a boat.

He had called Hope who was being observed in hospital at Inverness after getting a bad blow to the head, but she should be available soon. Ross would have to do for now. The detective was equipping himself well though and had most things in hand leaving Macleod free to think.

It was over an hour later when Macleod stepped ashore looking at the house he had fled for help earlier that day. A generator was being brought off the boat and lighting equipment to assist forensics as they worked into the night. Food was carried ashore too and large flasks of coffee, which Macleod felt like opening.

He was met at the door by the forensic officer who had been working on the bothy crime scene. He nodded politely and tried hard not to show he had forgotten her name.

"Hazel Mackintosh, DI Macleod. A joy as ever for both of us, I'm sure." The hoarse voice that sounded like cigarettes, and which had been the bane of her life, made it clear to Macleod she had read him easily.

"As ever," Macleod replied. "Anything yet?"

"Not really. But the body is not as badly burnt as the others were. Also the perpetrator left behind some of his fuel. There are canisters of petrol in there, which we can get matched up to other petrol if you can find me some samples from your suspects' houses. Might be worth a shot."

"Good," said Macleod, "I'll get Ross on to that. I think it was a man who attacked us because it felt like a big guy, and with the glimpses I got of his feet and legs, he seemed quite strong. Also, when he threw me, he didn't seem to struggle."

"I'll see what we can do. It's a funny place for someone to come."

"Not if you want to kill them. Away from anywhere, you

could probably take your time and dispose of the body easily. I wonder how many of our suspects knew about the place. Probably all of them, knowing my luck!" He felt in his pocket for his mobile to call in on Ross but pulled out a different one. "Hang on, this isn't mine." His mind raced then he remembered the fight. His mind must have been clouded because he should have remembered it. "Give me a bag, quick!"

Mackintosh shouted to a colleague and a bag appeared, into which Macleod dropped the mobile. Through the plastic he tried to activate it without success.

"Give it here," said Mackintosh and Macleod watched her fingers fly across the small keys as she encountered a password in the form of a drawn shape. "These are easy as everyone wants a shape they can remember." Macleod watched her trace the outside one way and then the other before working her way out from the centre. The screen changed to the home page.

"I'll dig up the telephone book," said Mackintosh. "Oh, hang on, 'Jim's phone,' it says here. And the phone book has an ICE."

"An ICE?"

"In case of emergency, number people call if they find your mobile when you're out on the floor. Says it's Alison Tunnock."

"I just came from there. He was as cool as a cucumber. The nasty swine, he's certainly big enough. I'll get Ross to get there and hold him, check his garage too for fuel. What do the canisters look like?"

"Green, pretty light and five litres only. And it's petrol, not diesel. That should be a starter until we can cross-analyse. I'll call the lab."

Macleod picked up his mobile and tried to ring.

"No signal, Inspector. Here!" Mackintosh threw him an

airwave radio, which he programmed to a channel Mackintosh suggested. He got hold of Ross and passed on the information he had discovered. But something was bothering him.

Anna Campbell was one thing. Maybe he had been over zealous, worried about her exposing him but what had he done? Had it been non consensual, had there been a fight? And why kill her anyway? His wife knew, after all. And what about the Carlton girl? He had gawked at them, he admitted that, but had he been involved? Maybe Missy would know. No, it wasn't sitting comfortably with him.

During the call Ross had said that information had come in about the cult the Carltons had been in but that the dossier was pretty thick. Macleod asked for a copy to be sent to Hope's mobile so she could look at it. Ross said he had spoken to her and she was good, just waiting to be let out. However, that would be in the morning at the earliest.

After wandering around the forensic site for an hour, during which Mackintosh told him to piss off but in a polite way, he took her advice and caught the boat back to Avoch where a car met him. He'd check in with Ross again and then go and see Hope. Before he could ring Ross, he had a call coming to him from the Inverness detective.

"Sir, we have found some of those canisters you talked about. In Tunnock's garage, just sat on the shelf. He said there are some missing, but I've arrested him and taken him to the station. He's denying everything, but you have his mobile and there's petrol missing so I thought it best to bring him in. I haven't charged him yet, though, waiting for your say-so."

"Good," said Macleod. "I'll see you at the station. And take some photographs of the canisters for me. I've seen the ones at the crime scene and can say if there's a match."

"Mackintosh already sent me pictures, sir. It's a definite match. I've got fuel samples for analysis."

At least we are getting somewhere, thought Macleod. I'll spin by the hospital before I go to the station, see what the gen is about the cult. She will be busting at the gut anyway, desperate to get back to it. And I'd better call Jane too at some point. But at least things are getting resolved, I might even get home within the week.

The driver of his car dropped him off at the hospital, which was handily across the road from the police station, and he made his way up several floors of the large building to a ward, which looked like every ward he had visited in hospital, clean but bland. Sterile maybe, but then that was the point, wasn't it?

As he entered the long white corridor, he was pulled aside by a nurse in scrubs who directed him to a side room. The woman was probably in her fifties and had the look of a stern senior nurse.

"She's had a bang to her head and she really needs to rest so don't go getting her excited and no getting her to sign herself out. Inspector, it was a heck of a blow and she needs rest."

Macleod was unsure how the woman had guessed he was an inspector but simply nodded as any debate would surely receive a chastisement. On entering the side room he was directed to, Macleod saw Hope sitting above her bed sheets with a mass of paper around her.

"Have you been talking about me?" he asked.

"Maybe." She laughed. "Did you get a word from Nurse Serious?" Macleod nodded. "Careful or she may spank your bottom." Hope pulled a rude look.

"I can see you're fine. We've arrested Jim Tunnock, there's

petrol matching the canisters in his garage and he dropped his mobile when he assaulted me. Makes sense he'd bump off Anna if he thought she'd drop stuff on him being around the first crime scene."

"If he was there. We may be dealing with two separate murderers or we may be being taken in by a sweet frame job. I don't get why he would kill Liberty Carlton. However, I do know why her father would kill her. This report from the states on the cult makes a heck of a read. These guys were hardcore before the authorities brought them down."

"In what way?"

"Well, I'd be dead for a start," said Hope. "Women had no real standing, property of their husband. They would dress as the husband wanted them to but would be kept covered if anyone else came round. Some of these women had some right hard bastards for husbands, kept them degraded all day. The woman were there to cook and clean, service their man. And they control the older girls' actions. Seems the boys were indoctrinated into this way of thinking and it just kept growing."

"So what happened over there?"

"Well, that's the thing, the Carltons got out just before the whole thing collapsed. Several daughters and wives were found dead, paper shoved in their mouths, killed because of affairs or even just dating outside the group. The Carltons left before everything kicked off, in fact about a week after the first girls went missing. But Justin was quite high up in the organisation by then."

Macleod walked to the window and looked out onto a vast car park. He saw people coming back and forth, some smiling, some in tears. Hospitals were places of such mixed emotions.

You had to be careful too; sometimes the best-hoped-for news was still rough to take, like the passing of a relative in pain. Seeing things for how they really were from the outside was hard here. Maybe it was hard in the case as well.

"We have no physical evidence against them, the Carltons I mean. I'll get the team over and check the place again. Jim Tunnock has a load of evidence against him, just missing a motive for the first murder."

"Unless he was seeing the girl. The man's a creep and he did spy on her, said she had a fit body."

"Standing and looking in the neighbours' back yard and seeing them flaunting where they shouldn't is no crime, and neither is enjoying the view. We need to talk to Missy or the mother to see if there was any involvement in that sense."

"My money is still on the father for the first murder. He's a bit psycho."

Macleod nodded. "However, he hasn't killed Missy, why not? She did more embarrassing stuff than her sister did. More things to hurt him. But she's actually in their house now. Photo on the wall, albeit covered up. Don't get me wrong, he's a strange one, but I do actually think he loves his family, just in a weird fashion."

"The shit is a pervert. You see the way he treats them. I mean if I was your daughter or wife would you have me parade around the house in next to nothing?"

Macleod looked at his partner as she sat up on her bed. Her legs were sticking out beyond her gown's end and her red hair was splayed across her shoulders. He knew the correct answer, but looking at Hope, he considered her question. You really can't ask your boss that. Not sat there like that.

"Of course not," said Macleod, maybe a little too quickly.

There was a short silence and he had to turn away to prevent his face from being read. "It's very wrong."

"Is that how you men think?"

Macleod turned around and raised his eyebrows. "It's kind of natural, Hope. Doesn't mean we have to act on it. But the thoughts are normal. You have no idea what we have to contend with."

Hope watched his face, gauging if he was serious. Then she laughed. Got away with that one, thought Macleod.

"So you need me in the interview?" asked Hope.

"You need to rest, Nurse Serious told me and I really don't want a spanking."

"You never used to be this forward," laughed Hope. "It's good, healthy. Have you called her today?"

"My private life is not up for debate."

"No then."

"When I get a moment." Macleod's face became suddenly grave. "We have a murderer to catch and if it's not Tunnock and it's the Carlton father, then a lot of immoral women as he sees it will be fair game. But I don't buy it, Hope."

"Check his place. Clothes, outbuildings for petrol and such."

"Of course. But I'll get hold of Missy too. Either way, tonight might be a long one. You enjoy your rest."

Macleod walked to the door and opened it before he heard Hope calling him.

"That's seriously a fantasy you have?"

Macleod nodded. "Of course, one of the milder ones." As he closed the door behind him he heard something hit it behind him. She thinks I'm joking.

# Chapter 16

Ross was a little surprised when Macleod told him to hold off on the interview with Tunnock. They had held him, he would ask for a brief no doubt and by then it would be the middle of the night. If Tunnock was the man they sought then they had him in custody, But if Hope was right then it would be a night with a killer on the loose and possibly eyeing up other targets.

His driver this time was a young constable, a blonde woman of maybe twenty-something. She was fresh and bright and had not long since come on shift. Occasionally she would glance at him and he found it a little disturbing. In fact, as the journey continued it was starting to bug him as she was doing it more and more.

"Is something wrong, Constable? Have I left my sandwich on the side of my mouth? Am I drooling? Have I suddenly acquired a lazy eye?"

The constable looked sheepish. "No, sir."

"Then what's up?"

"Well, it's just that you were the Inspector in charge on the Isle of Lewis, weren't you, when that woman and her son went in? You kept a body afloat and saved the girl they had kidnapped."

Macleod shook his head. "I didn't save the girl, Detective McGrath saved her, held the bag up in the water. She was the real hero."

"I knew that girl, sir. Went to the same school as her."

"Not difficult in Lewis. Or was it the same primary school as well?"

"Yes sir, the same primary school. Knew her fairly well."

"Okay," said Macleod, "but there's no need for the hero worship, we all do what we can. Be careful when we go in here as well. I know there are a lot of the boys about with us but some of these men don't like women, think you should know your place. They'd have you chained to the sink, dressed just for them." Macleod saw the look on her face. "I didn't say it was right, just letting you know that's where they are coming from. Don't go all moral either, we're not there to change the world, just to find a killer."

"Yes sir. I'll stay professional."

"I've no doubt you will, Constable, but it must be hard, especially for a woman, to see women kept like this. I don't like it as a man."

The car continued along the roads of the Black Isle and soon they had arrived at the Carltons'. The air was cold and crisp and Macleod looked at the snow around him as he made his way to the door. There was an officer on the door and Macleod asked him what had been going on.

"The family have been inside all day, sir. The young woman that arrived as well. We have remained at the door as requested. There's been activity out to the garage and they have been working in the field behind the house as well. But no one's come or gone from this front door." The officer stepped aside as Macleod rapped the door. He looked behind to his driver and saw a number of constables who had arrived in a separate car. The heavy squad in case it all kicked off.

The door opened and Mrs Carlton was standing in a coat that was wrapped up around her but not fastened with the provided buttons. She had the appearance of someone who had been disturbed and she looked grumpily at Macleod. "It's getting to bedtime, what's the matter now?"

For a woman who had been informed earlier that day that her daughter was dead, she seemed remarkably unaffected. "Pardon the intrusion, but I need to speak to Missy." Mrs Carlton nodded and invited him in before shouting up the stairs for Missy. The woman appeared at the top of the stairs in a tight roll-neck top and jeans, but as she descended her hair bounced clear of her face and Macleod saw the tears she had been crying. "My condolences, and my apologies for the intrusion, but I really need to talk to you."

"Of course, Inspector."

"Shall we walk outside?" Missy nodded and as Macleod turned away he watched Mrs Carlton remove her coat and walk back to the lounge. She was wearing underwear only and Macleod had to look twice to believe what he was seeing. Once outside, he questioned Missy on this.

"Is your mother unaffected by the news of your sister?"

Missy started to weep again. "She's a broken woman, doing just what Papa says. They see Liberty as getting her comeuppance. It's the price a disobedient woman pays. I had that all through my childhood and then teenage years. It's sick. But it is how she copes, goes back to what they know. That's why she's like that and Papa too. It's sick, isn't it?"

"I try not to comment on lifestyles, just criminal activity, but you are right, it's sick. Were your parents here all day?"

"As far as I could tell. I slept in the afternoon after hearing the news and have been upstairs all night."

Macleod nodded. "How well do you know Mr Tunnock next door?"

Missy sniffed and then laughed. "Binos Tunnock. He used to stand at his back window and watch us in the back yard as a family. All of us knew. Everyone except Papa. We didn't tell him as he would have gone over, probably killed the man. He certainly would have killed him if he had known what he got up to with me."

"How long ago was this?"

"Not long before I left. In fact, Inspector, he was the reason for me moving on. I had a bit of a fling with him but realised pretty quick I could do a lot better elsewhere."

"And did anyone know of this affair other than the two of you?"

"No." Missy paused, thinking. "Well, actually I think his wife knew or suspected but she never confronted me about it."

"Can we go to your garage? It's a bit nippy but I don't want to talk where any of your family can listen."

"Sure," said Missy and led Macleod round the side of the house and in through a side door in the building beside the house. "Do you think he killed my sister? Mr Tunnock?"

"Was your sister seeing him? Or had she been seeing him previously?"

"No, never. The dirty bugger wanted her, but I kept her clear, wanted him for myself in my own sad way. I never told her about Tunnock and me."

Macleod wandered along the garage and Missy switched on all the lights. In a far corner Macleod saw paint pots and clear bottles of a purple liquid. There were paint thinners and other solvents. And in the middle was one green canister. It was identical to the ones he had seen at the small house.

"What's the canister for?"

"Oh, that's Father's for his generator. He runs it down the far end of the farm if he needs lights to work at night. In fact, there're usually a lot more of them. I remember because he used to make me carry them down the land to the back. Can you imagine carrying one of those in a bikini, Inspector? Looked like something from an erotic farming calendar."

"I don't believe we have that particular variety in the station. How well do you know Anna Campbell?"

Missy gave a wry smile. "Anna, I know her, a soul who wanted the limelight that came with the celebrities. She was banging Andy MacTavish and wasn't so happy if he got it together with anyone else. She was jealous of me and Tunnock too, God help her. He told her about us, to tease her."

"She's dead. Killed at a place where I saw a lot of those canisters. When you say there should be more, how many does your father have here?"

Missy drew in her breath and Macleod could see her shake. "Six. Was always six."

One here, two at the house and three in Tunnock's. Hope might be right. "And tell me, if someone had a rolled up piece of paper in their mouth after they were dead would that have any significance to you?"

Missy bent over hyperventilating. "No, he wouldn't."

"Who wouldn't what?" insisted Macleod.

"Papa wouldn't kill them. He'd be angry, shout and yell, but he wouldn't kill them. Not like that."

"Like what?"

"The paper, the rolled-up paper. It tells God to abandon

them, to toss them in the Lake of Fire. It equates them to nothing, to shit. Scum, fornicators, the lowest of the low, to shit. Papa loves his family, whatever else you make of his madness, he loves us in his own way, he'd never do that to us."

"Are you sure?"

Missy was on her knees now, shaking physically, so much so that Macleod was worried for her health. "He taught us what the scroll in the mouth means. It's a separation of one person from another, abandoning them to the abyss. To a fate of pain and violence. That's beyond him to wish on us. I know because he didn't do it to me."

"I'm sorry," said MacLeod, "but I'm taking him in. There's too much stacking up against him in this case. I'm truly sorry for you."

# Chapter 17

"My own daughter, Macleod, that was my daughter. I couldn't do that to my own, I couldn't."

The words were haunting Macleod now as he stood on the Links at Cromarty, the small grass area that fronted the east side of the town. There was a cold nip in the air and he had contemplated simply going to bed, but something was bugging him. Hope's theory seemed correct, but when he had tackled Justin Carlton that night at the station, the man had been a mess. Sure, he had seen relatives deny any wrongdoing but the man was distraught. Everything inside of Macleod said that he hadn't committed the murders, which was unusual as Macleod hated what the man was. The way he had his girls dress, the whole domination attitude, it railed against Macleod's own developed sense of family.

Man was the head, that's what the Bible said, but not like that, to have your whim, to simply take from the woman. He was to love her, like Christ. And while that was no mean feat, it was so very far from Carlton's ways.

He watched the water as it rippled, so soothing. Turning around, Macleod made his way along the grass until he reached the now closed coffee shop, a wooden hut. Maybe he could grab a cup in the morning. Eight o'clock opening. He'd be well on the road by then. There was never enough time for things, even the beautiful but simple things.

He wandered down to the small concrete jetty that the three-car ferry came up to on the Cromarty side. Staring across at the Nigg yard, he watched the lights, shining like some Christmas storefront, giving him a sense of quiet industry. He had worked nightshift in his younger days and remembered that solidarity of just getting to morning and then finding a bed.

He thought he should ring Jane, she might be worried, but something inside didn't want to. Instead he looked at the water. What do you think, Hope? he asked, seeing the face of his dead wife before him. You never got to see this side of me, the calculating, ponderous soul I've become. I could have done with you being there, picking me up after a hard day staring at the bleak side of the human soul. Warm fire and a cuddle, maybe something more. We missed a lot of that, what we should have had. And then we missed kids, keeping us up, getting us up early. And we'll miss old age, watching our own making a hash of it like we did.

And what of this, Hope? Could you kill your own child for disobedience? His daughter didn't think so. But did she really know? Or was Carlton framed by Tunnock? But then why? Or was someone else playing silly buggers with the both of them?

I can still see you, sometimes. Getting into the shower is also a good time to see you. I remember that time I stepped in, not knowing you were inside. That was quite a time. I'm sorry about Jane, it's just I get lonely, I really do. But I can't let her in where you are because that would push you out. Two women can't have the same home, that's what my dad used to say. One's enough for one man. He was right, but I guess he meant living ones.

Macleod turned away again and followed the road beside the yachts sitting in the boatyard, out of the water for winter. A man with a dog passed and Macleod's "Hello" got an "Aye-aye" in response. He stared at the small harbour, at the work boats that bobbed about at the mooring. Maybe he should go somewhere quiet like this, out of Glasgow. Somewhere he didn't know anyone and they didn't know him. He could be an ordinary person, not responding to today's bad news. Maybe Jane would like it.

He wandered back to his accommodation and made himself a cup of instant coffee and turned on the television. When he saw himself making a statement to the press, he switched it off again. Why didn't they tell him his hair looked like that? Bored and restless, he got up, changed into his pyjamas and then sat in his dressing gown in front of a single-bar electric fire and took a book off the shelf. He was three chapters in when he realised he had no idea what he was reading or what it had said. Looking at the cover, it dawned on him that Interior Plumbing of the 19th Century was indeed as boring as the title suggested. He dropped the book on the floor.

Was he really waiting for forensics to come up with something? Papa had been at the house, but the locale was so near to the murders and the fact that Mrs Carlton was his sole alibi made the statement worthless. Tunnock had no clear alibi either. No, there was too much that was unclear.

His mobile rang and he looked at the screen. It was Jane. His hand wavered and then he picked the mobile up and pressed the accept button.

"Hi," said Macleod.

"Hey," said the soothing voice. "How are you?"

"Not great. Very tired."

"Okay, I'll not keep you."

"No, Jane, tell me about your day. Just talk to me." Macleod sat while she told him about something or other that had happened. He had no idea what she was saying as he was only listening to her voice. And then she spoke the immortal words. "Do you want me to come up?" There was silence.

"Well," Jane asked, "do you?"

"Honestly Jane, I don't know. I'm not good company. I'm wrapped up in this thing, it's bleak and it gets me down. I have to think about the blackest things. There's stuff you wouldn't want to hear and then there are all the things I can't talk about."

"Okay, Seoras. But you need to tell me. I'll get in the car right now if you need me, you hear me?"

"I know."

"Isn't Hope with you?" asked Jane.

"No. She's injured, getting out tomorrow."

"So, you're on your own, moping?"

"Yes," said Macleod.

"Go to bed, Seoras, but give me the address. I'll send something up."

"Okay. I'll do that."

Macleod quoted off the address on the small card in the living room and then said his goodbye to Jane. He couldn't invite her into this world. It was dark and horrifying. He took himself to bed and lay awake for another thirty minutes thinking through the case without making any headway. Then he turned over and fell asleep, exhausted.

It was almost four hours later when he heard the door opening below him. It was the front door and someone could be heard sneaking in and not making a good job of it. The tiredness in his body made him drift back to a low slumber, but when he heard the door handle turn, he suddenly froze in bed. If this was an intruder it was best to pretend to be asleep, especially while they were watching him. But then he heard the sound of clothes falling on the floor. He turned over in the bed and a sight caught his eyes that he would not forget. But then covers were thrown up and the figure climbed into the bed, wrapping two hungry arms around him.

"I felt you needed me, is that okay?"

"Oh yes," said Macleod. "It's so okay."

*********

Macleod awoke the next morning and felt behind him in the bed. No one was there. Rolling over, he checked with his eyes but again no one. There was a ruffle in the sheeting and the duvet was disturbed but it gave no real indication that someone had been there. Had he dreamt it all? No, Jane had been there, he had felt the warmth of her up against him.

He checked the digital clock in the room. Six o'clock. It wasn't even light outside. Macleod rolled his feet out of bed and grabbed his dressing gown. There was a sound, like something spitting, maybe sizzling in a pan. Opening the door, he smelt bacon, sausage and coffee. She was here, surely she was here. Or maybe Hope has discharged herself. No, bacon would not be on Hope's radar. Making his way downstairs he fought to wake his eyes up, rubbing them furiously. As he turned into the small kitchen he saw a pair of bare legs and a white shirt. There was a touch of cellulite running up the thighs but Macleod thought them to be a hot set of pins. He watched the shoulders and the brunette hair splayed across them as two hands worked a pan.

"You're up. I hope I didn't get you up, I tried to be as quiet as possible. I was going to make this for you and leave it in the oven while I went for a walk, but as you're up you might as well have it."

Macleod watched Jane turn around and place a plate on the table. Then she deposited every item she had in the pan before grabbing a coffee and leaving it beside the plate of steaming food. His eyes never hit the food but simply stared at her. The shirt was not done up and his jaw was hanging at the sight.

"If you drool, you are cleaning it up!" Jane said, laughing. But Macleod continued to stare at the flesh on show. "Shit, Seoras, is Hope about? I thought she was in hospital, not due out. Did she get out early?" Jane began wrapping the shirt around her as tight as she could.

"No, she's still in hospital. Its just, well, you know." Jane shook her head. "Been a long time since a woman cooked me breakfast standing half naked. The last time was my Hope, you are so darn like her.

"Glad to know I still have it," said Jane and allowed the shirt to drop back to its more provocative position. She let Macleod sit down and then plonked herself in his lap. "I didn't bring my own gown, forgot it in the rush, so I grabbed a shirt of yours. I thought you wouldn't mind."

"Trust me, I don't," said Macleod, his hands disappearing inside the shirt.

"As good as that is," replied Jane, "you need to eat that before it gets cold. I'm going to have a shower."

"Do you have to get dressed?"

"I never said anything about getting dressed."

Macleod watched Jane disappear out of the kitchen and blew out a long breath. Wow, just incredible. He imagined her entering the shower as he tucked into his breakfast. The egg was a little overdone but he was not about to complain. He wolfed the food down and swiftly washed it away with his coffee. Wondering how long she would be, he decided to join Jane in the shower but then heard her leaving the bathroom. Her footsteps sounded like heaven as she came down the stairs before entering the kitchen in the same shirt she had been wearing, except now it had wet patches where she had not dried well.

"When do you have to be in?" asked Jane.

"Never," replied Macleod.

"No, really."

"I can take an hour."

"Good," said Jane, approaching and then straddling his knees. She filled his entire view and Macleod was lost in a joy that had been too devoid from his life. Jane suddenly jumped up.

"What the heck's that? Your pocket."

Macleod felt the vibration of his mobile and cursed inwardly. Why now, for Pete's sake, why now? "Sorry," he apologised and held up the mobile to his ear.

"Macleod here!" He was still looking at Jane standing beside him and his displeasure roared through his answer.

"Morning sir, Ross here. We have a problem. Jimmy Mochilas is missing. Been missing since last night. Was reported about four o'clock, but I wanted to confirm it before I got you up. His car is in a layby on the A9. Door was open, seems he may have been pulled from the vehicle. There's also blood at the scene, not a lot but maybe enough for an injury."

Damn, damn, damn. "Okay Ross, you got someone who can pick me up?"

"Ten minutes, sir. That okay?"

"That's fine, Ross." Macleod switched the mobile off and placed it in his pocket. "Someone missing, Jane. I have to go."

"Is this common? Am I to expect you to concoct these excuses when I try to get closer?"

"No. I'm not running. It's the job, it's just that…" Macleod saw she was laughing.

"I know it is but your face. This isn't a one-off," she said, kissing him on the forehead. "You get to inspect me anytime." With that she walked to the door. Macleod watched her depart and then remembered he needed to get changed. As he walked to the door, it opened again. "But just to let you know, as you are going out, I am going to bed. I don't drive half the night for any man then parade like this for his delight. It's only you, Seoras. I want you, and I don't care what it takes."

Macleod walked forward and slipped his hands under her shirt again.

"Hey, hands off. You have work and I'm not taking any half measures. I'll be here when you get back."

"I don't know how long I'll be. I genuinely don't."

Jane looked at him. "I said I'll be here, okay? We ain't finished."

Macleod watched her disappear again and then thought how she was going back up to his room where his clothes were. And he chased her up the stairs.

# Chapter 18

The A9 layby was cordoned off and one side of the road closed to traffic, which had caused a holdup on what was a busy route for the Highlands. Macleod stood in his jacket, surrounded by snow but currently had his feet walking through a pile of slush. The road surfaces were clear but the layby had not had the same treatment. Thankfully, he had his wellingtons on, but that meant his feet were cold, missing the snug fit of his shoes.

"Have we any further details, Ross?"

The sergeant pulled his notebook from his jacket pocket. The man was not wearing a jacket and Macleod thought him either immune to the cold or simply insane. "Happened about three o'clock this morning. We had a driver pass by about two forty-five and the open door and car were then spotted at ten past three and called in. Both travellers were on their way to distant parts and have seemingly no connection to Mochilas."

"Any cars seen?"

"No, sir. We're looking at partial tracks but, given the layby is used quite often and it had a slush formed rather than snow, the imprint will be awkward, so not sure if we'll get anything."

Macleod sniffed the droplet of water off his nose. He was starting to feel chilly and remembered how Jane was waiting back at the little rented house. He preferred the view he had that morning to this. "Any details on Mochilas' last movements before this?"

"Worked at the radio station yesterday morning, made his statement at our station; after that, it appears he was at the leisure centre playing badminton. Left there about ten o'clock and his car was at his house at midnight according to a neighbour. They didn't hear him leave."

"Good work, Ross. Anyone been to the radio station? I'd like to know where the staff were last night and early hours of this morning. We have three bodies. We've been thinking this is a romantic killing, offended father, but this is a bit strange. I want to be sure there's nothing happening at the radio station."

"I'll get someone down right away, sir. Also had a call from Detective McGrath saying she's ready to come out of hospital. Shall I send a car for her?" asked Ross.

"No," said Macleod, "I'll get her. Was there any mobile or diary or anything in the car?"

"Just condoms, sir. Two packets."

"Makes sense he was entertaining in the car. Makes me wonder if this is revenge for his playing about. Maybe something else…" Macleod stroked his chin, deep in thought.

"Sir?" asked Ross.

"Nothing Sergeant, let's get on, shall we? Oh, thank you." Macleod had just been handed a large coffee in a paper cup complete with lid.

"It's just black, sir. Sorry but we didn't know how you took it," said a uniformed officer.

"It's perfect," said Macleod, taking a sip of the steaming coffee. He said his farewell to Ross and then got in a car and headed for the hospital.

The day had begun at the city hospital and as Macleod walked across from the car park to the main entrance, the place was abuzz with staff and visitors. The coffee had warmed him up and as he entered the corridor where he had previously met his first informant's partner in the small shop, Macleod heard a shout. Turning around he spotted Hope sitting in the cafe. She was smiling, her red hair tied up behind her, a casual jacket hung around her shoulders and a white body underneath. Her jeans were dark and complemented her boots. While she looked the part, Macleod thought he saw something underneath.

"Hey, you okay?" he asked.

"Ready for duty," said Hope.

"That's not what I asked. Are you okay?"

"I think so, little shell-shocked at getting clobbered like that. We were lucky. We could have ended up lying there dead. You certainly saved the day."

Macleod shook his head. "You and me don't keep score. Glad to see you though. Has Ross sent you any details about the kidnap?"

Hope nodded. "Seems strange, I'm not sure where to place Mochilas in all this. We know he's ambitious, happy to take on a married woman, thinks himself better than most. I would say snubbed lover but this seems strange. Kidnapped from a layby. Dragged from a car. He wasn't that small."

"Couple of minutes in the middle of the night. Kidnapped, so it's not a chance stopping, I reckon."

Hope coughed. "Are we sure he's alive? This isn't another killing?"

"There was blood but it was minimal. Nothing identifying or giving us a timescale left, not a note or phone. Seems almost semi-professional. Anyway, come on, I'm going over to the radio station, see if anyone heard anything. We have our believed killer in custody, which makes this strange. Either we are wrong or someone is using this as cover. I also want to see who is doing the breakfast show today. They seem to be running out of options."

Together they crossed to the car and left the hospital for the nearby radio station. Macleod let Hope drive and he tried to look at her head wound on the rear of her cranium without her noticing, but he was up against a police woman.

"You can just take a look if you want. Gently mind, it's still sore."

Macleod cautiously pushed back the hair and saw the stitching around McGrath's wound. "They made it neat anyway. Give it a week."

"I'll live."

The car pulled up outside the radio station and Macleod saw a young man on the reception desk who approached him as Macleod entered. The man was neat and wearing a suit.

"Hi and welcome to the station, can I help you?"

"Temp?" queried Macleod. The man nodded. Pulling out his ID, Macleod asked to see the station manager but was advised that she hadn't been in yet today.

"Has anyone passed the news of the kidnap on to her?"

The man shook his head sullenly and then thought. "Should I do that?" he asked.

"No," said Macleod, "I'll do it." He walked past the man and opened the door to the corridor with the studios. Peeking in, he saw a girl broadcasting, fairly young, at least compared to him. "Who's that?"

"Oh, that's Shona Hibbert, does the through-the-night show.

She stopped on."

Macleod nodded before looking around a little further. He wasn't sure what he wanted but he knew this temporary receptionist was not going to find out for him. Then his mobile rang.

"Macleod!"

"Ross here. We have dashcam footage and have identified the van. It's a rental but the rental office had CCTV and I got a look at the image. It's the Savage brothers. We're just going to pay them a visit, they run a funeral home."

"Should I know them?" asked Macleod.

"No, sir, small time. Nasty but nothing that usually ends up fatal. GBH is more likely. I've texted the address. If you're at the station you are not far."

"On my way," said Macleod, grabbing Hope's arm and dragging her behind him.

The drive to the funeral home took them across the mouth of the River Ness, where it emptied out through lock gates to the sea. Following a small track, Macleod saw a police car up ahead and joined the two officers already on scene.

"All closed up," said a blonde-haired, female police constable. "We asked around and there's a river cruise company just down hiring boats for the Caledonian Canal. Apparently the Savage brothers took one. There was a woman with them, sketchy description as she stayed outside the whole time."

"Got a name for the boat?"

"Melody Jane, apparently. Motor cruiser, can take five people." The constable smiled up at Macleod and he gave an encouraging smile back. He turned away and rang Ross.

"Ross? They are on the loch by the looks of it. Let's keep this low key, no uniform as we don't want to spook them. Get some plain cars to sweep the loch from the roadside and see if we can spot the motor cruiser Melody Jane. The brothers are on it with a woman. I'm on the west side of the canal so I'll start down here with McGrath, see what we can see."

After telling the constables to check back in with their station, Macleod and McGrath drove the car down the main road along Loch Ness. Ross had sent through a picture of the Savage brothers and Macleod studied it as Hope drove. As they reached the side of the main stretch of Loch Ness, Hope pulled the car over. She went to exit the car but Macleod grabbed her arm. He took off his tie and then grabbed a pair of binoculars.

"Let's make this look like a couple of tourists. Follow me out in a minute." Macleod exited the car and stood in just his shirt on the lochside. He raised up his binoculars, scanning the loch, and picked out a few boats. One was a yacht, another a cruiser but it was smaller than what he was looking for. The name was also wrong. Then he saw another one. The side of the vessel read "Janet Marie."

A pair of arms wrapped themselves around him and he felt Hope's breath on his neck. She was jacketless too and the press of her body nearly caused him to lose concentration. "Over there," he whispered, nodding at the vessel he was looking at.

Hope took the binoculars off him and then casually looked up and down the loch before focusing briefly on the vessel again. "Right size, wrong name though."

"The name's in the wrong place. It looks wrong," said Macleod. "Let's get back in the car."

"Get the camera," said Hope, "I think someone's coming on deck."

Macleod retreated to the car and picked a camera from the boot. Hope stood on the wall by the loch, holding her head up as Macleod zoomed the camera in and got a shot of the person on deck. The distance was long but it was the best they could do.

Getting back into the car, Hope transferred the picture to her mobile and sent the image to Ross. A text came back promptly.

Unsure of the vessel but the figure looks like Iain Savage and I reckon that's his girl. Cannot be one hundred percent sure, but if I was a gambling man, I'd say it was him.

# Chapter 19

Soon there was a covert operation running, watching the vessel Janet Marie. Unaware of whether anyone was on board, Macleod was reticent to simply storm his way over onto the boat but he was also painfully aware that there was a killer abroad and needing to be dealt with. In either case, the only people spotted on board had been the Savage brothers and now one of them was taking a tender and looking to make his way to the side of the loch.

"He's not making for any known jetty," said Hope. "It looks like he's just going to ditch it."

"Okay, then let's see where he goes. There's no guarantee Mochilas is on the boat, he may be hidden elsewhere and they only conducted the kidnap and are now staying low. Get in a car and follow him, McGrath, I'll keep an eye on things here. But keep in touch."

Hope nodded and immediately pointed at a plain clothes officer, asking for the keys to his car. Together, they got in and drove towards the spot Savage was heading for. Hope found herself boxed between a blue van and a green hatchback but patiently waited for the traffic to progress along. As they neared the spot where Savage was seemingly coming ashore, the blue van in front pulled over to one side. Hope drove on past but she saw in her rearview mirror that the blue van was opening its side door.

"He's jumped in that van and they look like they are turning around towards Inverness," Hope told her colleague in the car. "Get another plain car to come up towards us and I'll swap over."

Sure enough, a plain car had pulled over a little way back from the spot where the blue van had taken Savage on board. Hope pulled her car over before exchanging her ride for the other car. Soon she was sat in the passenger seat directing a blonde female officer to pursue the blue van.

Eyes glued to the windscreen, Hope encouraged her colleague on until she glimpsed the van going around a corner. "Tail him," she cried and the constable increased the speed on her car. The vehicle continued on its way into Inverness where the constable had to drive carefully so as not to get too close to the other traffic. At a set of lights on the edge of the town, Hope saw Savage jump out and make his way to a bus stop.

"Get round the corner out of sight and drop me off, I'll tail him on foot."

Taking the car off the main road at the next junction, the constable slowed the car down and allowed Hope to exit. She immediately spun around and walked back towards the bus stop she had seen Savage at. As she turned the corner, she saw a bus arriving and Savage getting on. She was a good distance from it and began to sprint towards the bus. The bus began to move off and Hope quickened her pace, going full out to stop it. There was a risk that Savage would see her but she needed to take it.

Fortunately, the bus driver had to stop suddenly as a car pulled out in front of him. Hope arrived at the front door and banged on it. The man inside shook his head, pointing back at the stop. Hope pulled her credentials and held them to the window. The door opened and Hope quickly put her identification away. She pulled out some change but the driver shook his head. Hope placed the money down anyway.

"Take it and give me a ticket. Not a word to anyone."

The driver punched in a fare and Hope ripped off the ticket. Walking along the bus, she spied Savage sitting in the rearmost seat on the same side as the driver. This was good as he may not have seen her efforts to get on board. Hope took up a seat in the middle of the bus and fought the urge to look round. Instead, she took out her mobile and texted Macleod her position and the situation. Ring me came the text reply.

Taking an earpiece out from her jacket pocket, Hope attached it and then dialled Macleod's number. After a few rings it was answered.

"Macleod!"

"Hi," said Hope, "I was wondering if you could help me, I need help finding a place. I have something with me that is definitely going to be in this new room but I need to think about where exactly I want to live."

"Good, so you still have him," said Macleod. "Is he on his own?"

"Yes, but who knows if that will stay the same once we get our own place."

She could almost hear Macleod thinking. "Stick close. I'm not sure how Justin Carlton is running this as we have him at the moment. I'm going to find out if any of the family know the Savages. If he meets anyone or if he goes to a final spot, then let me know. Otherwise keep a distance."

Hope switched off the call and put the earpiece away.

Macleod was right, how was Carlton running this? Or was this planned some time ago? It was becoming a bit awkward. Could it be about the radio personnel instead? But then what did the paper in the mouths really mean? The cult in America attached meaning to it but then maybe someone else also did.

After twenty minutes, Savage walked past her pressing the red button beside Hope to signal he wished to get off. Behind him, Hope stood up and followed him off the bus. She then let herself fall behind until she had Savage only barely in her sights.

They were in a quiet part of town and Hope watched Savage sit down in an outdoor seat at a small cafe. He was looking around him as she watched from an alleyway. She scanned the houses across from Savage and then chose to walk to an older looking building with net curtains in the windows. She rapped on the front door and then waited until an elderly woman opened the door.

"Hello, I'm with the police and I need to look out your window, ma'am. Please invite me in and I'll show you my ID."

The woman was small and frail and she struggled to lift her head to see Hope. Gently, Hope took her hand and led her inside, closing the door behind her. The woman became panicked and Hope had to produce her credentials and let the woman telephone the local station. Meanwhile, Hope watched through the net curtains until her mobile rang again. Macleod said that he was concerned as they couldn't find Missy when they looked to question the family. He said he was ready to move against the boat given that two people were missing and were potentially on it.

Looking out of the window again, Hope told him to hang on

as someone was now sitting across from Savage. The day was cold and the woman shivered despite the large grey coat she had on. Hope took a scarf out of her jacket and tied it round her head. Then she took her jacket and reversed it. Wearable with either side in or out, she had bought the jacket for this express purpose but this was the first time she had tried it.

Telling the old woman to stay inside, she exited and then crossed over to the cafe where Savage was sitting with the woman. She had sunglasses on despite the weather and had pulled her jacket up close to her as she spoke to Savage. Hope overheard, "That will be on you," but little else. She lingered hoping to hear the woman speak but she was saying little.

"How long do we need to keep him to make it real?" asked the woman and she was told another two days at least.

Hope stepped briefly inside and ordered a coffee, taking it outside to the other free table at the cafe. She felt frozen but at least she was safely within listening distance. There was a conversation about the package; how well it was, what had it eaten, was it distressed? The voice of the woman was familiar and Hope struggled to place it. She examined the footwear and also recognised them.

A large envelope passed between the two parties causing Savage to smirk. "Good," he said, "the rest when we release him. Pity you can't see him. Hope the breakfast show is going okay."

That was it. The station manager Laura Tulloch, it was her. The shoes were classy, and the look, but that voice was the real giveaway.

"He's okay, Mrs Rose, we'll let him go in a wee while, a few days. And, no, you won't hear from us again. I'll go now."

Hope peeled away from her table and watched Savage walk

off. She then sat down at the place Savage had used and looked up into the woman's shades.

"Evening Mrs Tulloch, been wanting you today but you were out. May I know what this conversation was about?"

There was silence, before a curt, "I have nothing to say."

Hope's mobile rang. It was Macleod. Missy Carlton was missing. When they had called the family together, she was gone. All the rest were present. Hope wondered what it meant but she told Macleod about Laura Tulloch. As she was getting nowhere she thought maybe he should just storm the boat.

# Chapter 20

Macleod licked his lips in the dry air. He had a cold sore coming on and he blamed it on the weather up here at Inverness. Or maybe it was the stress. People forgot that. As much as this was his day job and he was used to the business, he still felt stress like any constable, paramedic or other emergency worker. And when the case was on, the stress was usually at its height.

So Laura Tulloch had met the Savage brother. And Missy Carlton was missing. Ross had called and Macleod had had to clarify what he meant by missing. She had not been seen that day. Her bed had not been slept in, her car was missing. Her mother had no idea where she had gone. With Carlton locked up, there had been no officer on the door either. Dammit.

He looked over at the boat, bobbing on the water, an anchor line holding it in its current locale. It all seemed wrong. Why on earth was the boat here? Why would you suddenly kidnap and hold Mochilas after killing off the others at the two bothy houses? And Mochilas' link to it all was tenuous. Carlton didn't have him, Carlton was in a cell. So if Carlton did it he had accomplices. And the car left on the A9, the DJ snatched. So very different.

Missy's disappearance was more in keeping with the murders. If only they had grabbed the killer when they followed Anna Campbell, then things would be done and he'd be back in Glasgow, cementing his relationship with Jane. Instead he was having to run from her to deal with all this.

Macleod stroked his chin. Laura Tulloch, the woman who said she never did anything like this. Was she part of the Mochilas kidnap? Was she involved in the killings? He found it hard to believe. Were there two different strands running here that had crossed?

Liberty Carlton had been seeing Andy MacTavish, and then they were found dead together at their secret meeting place. Anna Campbell, also linked to Andy MacTavish in the past, a friend of Liberty, murdered going to meet someone. Pieces of paper in their mouths all giving the indication of a cult. Fuel for the fires found at Carlton's. Surely it was him. But now people were still going missing when Carlton was locked up.

Jim and Alison Tunnock, fuel at their house, but surely that was a setup. They had no reason to make things get this dark. They were unhappily running affairs, each aware of the other. Why kill these other people?

The station seemed to be a hotbed of scandal and complaining, but to kill for a job? Why take out the rest? Mochilas was maybe jealous and looking for a job promotion, but it was a bit much. He wasn't doing that badly at the station. And Laura Tulloch, the woman who didn't do things like that. Maybe, but what did things like that stretch to?

Carlton's own daughter though. And now another missing. Could Carlton really bring himself to dispatch his girls? The thing was that while he had them dress up in lingerie and whatever else, he genuinely seemed to love them. Missy left and he did nothing. He didn't keep them indoors and forbid them to mix with the outside world completely, despite the contamination that would surely bring. Maybe he's a victim then. Maybe it's all too simple.

Macleod grabbed his mobile. "McGrath, have you still got Laura Tulloch in sight? Good, bring her in. I'll meet you at the Inverness station."

Macleod gave instructions for the boat to be watched and for him to be updated. He'd need to move soon on the boat but he wanted to be sure. Even if the Savage brothers were involved, he wanted to know where his victim had gone. Just because someone grabbed someone didn't mean they were taking over the feeding and watering of a victim. And also why kidnap and hold? The murderer never did that before.

A half hour later, he was sitting in the interview suite awaiting Hope. Macleod had instructed Ross to keep an officer up at the Carltons' until further notice, also to be aware of any phone calls and where they came from. The coffee was warm but only just and he had finished the mug by the time Hope arrived. They entered interview room one where an indignant Laura Tulloch was filing her nails.

"I have a station to run, Inspector, and this is a disgrace."

"No it isn't, it's an investigation and I have three bodies on my hands and people missing. So I want to know why you were meeting with Ronald Savage today? What was the topic of conversation?"

Laura Tulloch gave Macleod a scowl and then swept her hair to one side and pursed her lips. "If you must know, old times. Ronald was at school with me and, to be frank, was my first. He's always held a candle for me and I for him. With all that's been happening, I just fancied some time with someone appreciative."

Macleod shook his head. “How did you go to school with Savage? You’re not from here.”

“Neither is he, he’s from Brighton like me, moved up here a while back now. Maybe fifteen years.”

“And what?” asked Hope. “You just ran into him?”

“Oh, no, we’ve always kept in touch. Always good to keep in touch with a man who has certain—” she flashed her eyes and gave a quick breath like something was scalding her “—skills.”

“He has skills. Extortion, GBH, all sorts of thuggery on his record.”

“That’s not the skills I was referring to, Inspector.”

Macleod flushed and was delighted when Hope interrupted. “But you weren’t discussing how he could jack you off best when I was listening to your conversation.”

Jack you off? She’s so damn crude.

Hope continued, “You were talking about releasing someone. Who?”

Laura Tulloch calmly sat back in her chair. “Pigeon racing. Apparently Ron’s a big fan of it, thinking about getting some. Which is fine as long as he doesn’t let them near me, poo everywhere.”

“Enough,” said Macleod. “Who have you kidnapped? Where have you put them?”

Her eyelids blinked and her lips caved in slightly at the word them. Macleod thought for a moment. How much should he say? He might just overplay his hand so she knew everything but then it would be harder to trap her or get a conviction.

“Are they together?” A furrow appeared on Laura Tulloch’s brow. “This will link to the murders, so you’d better come clean or the book will be thrown at you.”

Hope touched Macleod’s shoulder and he looked at her to

find eyes asking if she could take over. Did she see it too? Macleod nodded his assent.

"How're ratings? Plenty of people listening. You said they had dropped when Andy MacTavish was on. Were they improving with Mochilas? With all the commotion it should be a great pull to your station."

Hope continued to stare at Laura who seemed to be deep in thought. Then she shifted in her chair, turning her hips and leaning forward towards Macleod. He noticed her blouse dip and she made no attempt to cover up the view.

"That's not going to work," said Macleod. "Just tell me what I need to know."

"Do I get a deal for owning up?"

"A deal?" Macleod went red in the face. The cheek of the woman. "There're three dead, I'm trying to let you clear your name of those deaths not organise a picnic. Tell me what your involvement is right now."

Laura Tulloch straightened up but kept her focus on Macleod. She leaned forward again and Macleod found himself looking involuntarily at her cleavage. He stood up and turned away. "Enough. I'll tell it for you, shall I?"

He kept his back to Laura and glanced down at Hope who was smiling broadly. "You told me that you weren't into any nasty business at the station, had nothing to do with Andy McTavish's death. I heard you say that the first time and do you know what I thought?" The question hung for a moment.

"Bullshit!" said Hope.

Macleod glanced at Hope who was smiling at Laura and seemed pleased with her comment. Nonsense, what is wrong with the word nonsense? Why's everything a swear word? "As my colleague says, nonsense! I think you liked the fact that he was murdered and thought it was going to give your station a boost. But maybe it hasn't worked too well or maybe it did. Then Anna Campbell is murdered and that's another worker of yours in the news. The new boy on the breakfast show is good but this would be a chance to establish him, really hold him up."

"So you make some news," said Hope, interrupting. "You make it up by getting hold of an old thug-cum-boyfriend and get him to hold on to your guy. What was the deal after that? Was the station to pay a ransom? Was he to escape on his own?"

"On his own," said Laura Tulloch dismissively. "We can't have the station involved. Two weeks away he was getting. Tied up but nothing too dramatic, simply out of the way and then escaping by Loch Ness, a little swim to shore. And then back on the show, a hero. I was setting him up for the next few years. He should really thank me."

"Ring Savage," said Macleod. "Tell him to bring the boat to the nearest jetty and we'll bring everyone in. They are being watched."

"Can we not have a bit of a moment? You could storm onto the boat, maybe have a few people fall in and then a chase to shore." Laura Tulloch leaned forward again, licking her lips delicately along her red lipstick. Evil, thought Macleod, that's just plain evil. She'd trap too many a man.

"Call now," said Macleod, "and end this quickly. You are being charged and I will throw the book at you because I have a killer on the loose and you are frankly wasting my time."

"Now, now, Inspector, surely we can come to an arrangement?" Again the cleavage and the look of extras to follow. Macleod was disgusted.

"McGrath, deal with this. Get that boat back in and everyone tucked up in the cells. Tell Mochilas what his boss has done for him. See if he appreciates it. You can meet me when you are done with this..."

"Bullshit?" offered Hope.

He had to leave very quickly. Outside the door of the interview room, he placed a hand over his mouth to stop from laughing. Hope was so good at that, getting him to find her vulgarity funny. Taking a moment to compose himself, he was interrupted by a constable.

"Inspector," said the young man, "I've been asked to find you. Mr Carlton's lawyer says that they need to speak to you. Said his client is willing to confess to the murders. Also to the kidnappings. But his lawyer said they need to move fast otherwise things will not work out. He said Missy may be dead soon if he can't rescind his instructions."

# Chapter 21

Macleod raced to the second interview room that held Justin Carlton and his lawyer. He found Carlton biting on his fingernails and frantically looking from left to right. Beside him dressed immaculately in a dark suit with a white blouse was a short brunette woman, maybe in her thirties and with glasses that spoke of business. Taking the seat in front of the table the couple were sitting behind, Macleod placed his hands on the table.

"Why is Missy in trouble? Why will she be dead?"

"Because I ordered it. She'll be finished very shortly." Carlton looked at the wall as he spoke.

"Where, by whom and when?"

Macleod saw Hope sit down beside him and leaned back into his seat.

"My associate. He's going to kill her on my instruction. Give me a phone and I'll stop it."

Macleod stared at Carlton who shuffled in his seat. "Who are you phoning?"

"I won't say. But I will call him and make sure it doesn't happen." Carlton was shaking nervously.

"My client is offering to help, Inspector, to stop the death of an innocent, may I suggest you act on it?" The woman made a point of looking over her glasses at Macleod as if any other course of action would be the dumbest act ever perpetrated by man.

“Sorry, ma’am, your name?”

“Janice Kyleholm, Mr Carlton’s lawyer.”

“Okay Miss Kyleholm. Firstly, if someone’s going to be killed we need to be there to prevent it. Secondly, why are you calling us in? Surely you could just have given Mr Carlton your phone and stopped it? All he would have to do was tell his partner to run. Why bother with us?”

“Because,” said the woman sharply, “Mr Carlton is doing the right thing and involving you. He’s trying to stop any further hurt.”

“And he’s admitting to the three murders so far, including that of killing his own daughter? You’re telling me he killed his own daughter?”

“That’s exactly what we are saying.”

“Mr Carlton,” asked Macleod, “did you kill your daughter Liberty?”

Carlton nodded his head.

“We’re still on tape, can you give me a yes for the tape?” asked Macleod. He watched the man lift his head, his eyes streaming with tears. But the man remained silent. “I need you to say it.”

“Say yes for the tape,” advised Miss Kyleholm. “It’s just a formality the detective is asking for.”

“A formality,” yelled Carlton, his face now red and his eyes flowing with tears. “My daughter’s death a fucking formality. She’s dead, you hear that? She’s dead.”

“Yes she is,” said Hope, “but from talking to your girls, they say you wouldn’t have hurt any of them. That’s not what you do.”

"But I … I … did it." The voice was a hoarse whisper.

"Say again, louder for the tape," said Hope.

"I just said it."

"Then say it again, for the tape, louder," indicated Macleod.

"I think my client has said it well and proper…"

"No, he hasn't," said Macleod. "We need it on the tape."

"Okay … okay," whimpered Carlton, "I did it, I killed her. I killed Liberty! Was that loud enough?"

"Loud enough, but I doubt it's accurate," said Macleod.

The tension in the room was palpable and Macleod felt his palms sweating. Beside him, he saw his partner almost rock back and forth on her seat. Something was bothering Macleod though. Carlton had said the words but he still seemed nervous, like he was hiding something else.

"Tell me how you did it," asked Macleod.

"Well … well … I burnt them to death, used my fuel."

"Why?"

"Because she was sullied, being with that bastard, so I killed them both."

"Anything else about the deaths? Did you leave any other signs or marks?"

Macleod watched Carlton's face suddenly light up and then his face went into a look of horror.

"The rite, I did the rite."

"What rite?" asked Hope.

"I placed two scrolls in their mouths."

"Why?" asked Hope. "Surely they would have burned up."

"The scrolls lock their souls out of heaven. She had to pay a punishment. She had to…" Carlton broke down, inconsolable. But something was chiding at Macleod.

"So why use someone else this time? What's so different?"

"Well, I'm in here."

Got me there, thought Macleod. But something is still wrong.

"Why now though? Missy has been off and walking around on her own for ages. You could have killed her first instead of Liberty." Here Carlton broke down in tears again.

"What more do you want, Inspector? You have my client's confession. Another tick in your box."

Macleod stood up quickly, so much so that the table was bumped into the air before settling. Tick in the box, he thought, you cheeky madam. No, there's something going on here, he's protecting someone.

"Who's doing the killing?"

The man collapsed to the floor and Hope raced round ready to offer assistance. But the man was merely crying on the ground, his shoulders shaking.

Macleod stood to his full height. "Frankly, Mr Carlton, I don't believe you. You have never harmed one of your children and you haven't started this year. Come on, Hope, I think we are done here."

Carlton picked himself up off the floor. "No, don't! She'll be dead. She'll not stand a chance. He may even have her. There's no time."

"Who?" yelled Macleod. "Tell me who or I will walk out of here." From the corner of his eye, he saw the worried look on Hope's face.

Carlton began to cry again, his shoulders shaking with a pain he was struggling to contain. Macleod stood impassively and once again saw Hope staring at him wide-mouthed.

"Fine, if you have no name then we are done here."

"Am I free to go?" Carlton asked through a cracking voice.

"No! We are not done with you yet. You've just confessed to three murders; I can't let you walk out of here. We'll be back later tonight. I have work to get on with." As he turned on his heel, Hope was on her feet coming over to him. "Not now, McGrath, outside."

As he stepped out the door, Hope in tow, Macleod heard the screams of the man in torment. "Okay," yelled Carlton, "Ven will kill her. Ven will do to Missy just what he did to Liberty. He'll leave the note, she'll not see heaven. Do you understand? She won't see heaven!"

Macleod gave a thin grin. He had known it. "McGrath, radio the officers at the house to arrest Ven Carlton and bring him to the station. We need to talk to him."

Twenty minutes later, Macleod was standing in an alcove near the coffee machine in the station when Hope approached him. She had a determined look about her, like she was about to ferret out the truth whatever he thought about it. Her head tilted slightly and her tone softened as women did when wanting to get something from a man. He doubted it was intentional, just as a man changes his tone to impress or suggest something to a woman.

"How did you know?"

"Know what?" asked Macleod. But he was teasing, he knew what she meant.

"Carlton. The father. How did you know he didn't do it?"

"Man's intuition."

Hope laughed. "Piss off … sir."

Macleod smiled. "Maybe it's a man thing, maybe not. When you look at Justin Carlton, what do you see?"

"Sexist pig. Kept his wife and daughters in a state of perverted bliss for him. Constantly paraded before him and yet kept from normal male relationships. Owned and kept. He obviously didn't think much of them." The look of disgust on Hope's face was clear to see.

"Wrong, you've let your prejudices get ahead of you. Although I don't blame you." Macleod saw the look of shock on Hope's face. "You need to see it from his angle. This cult, from its point of view, esteemed women. Yes, they were for a husband's pleasure but he was also there to keep and love them. His duty was to make sure they were not abused. Someone running off for a spot of how's your father with his daughter was a horror, an abomination. But to them, to have these woman who they saw as beautiful walking around in not a lot was normal, the way it should be. Remember he was never abusive."

"But they had marks on them, one of the girls had marks on them." Hope was indignant.

"Yes they did. But not what they would see as abuse. Simply a rebuke to keep them on the straight and narrow. Like the smack of a child, at least how it was seen. Normal for Carlton was a happy family, kept safe from the world and able to parade their beauty within safe environments."

"You actually believe that?" asked Hope. "Is it your upbringing making you agree?"

Macleod held up his hand and took a long drink of his coffee. "Easy Hope, I never said I agreed, I was just getting inside his head. But don't just blame him, Precious Carlton believes in it too. She's been back here and could have run. Whether she's brainwashed to it or simply believes it I don't know, but she is certainly complicit to it now.

"You see Missy ran away and Carlton did nothing. We know that the cult they were in would have demanded she die and then have the paper put in the mouth to stop their soul ascending to heaven or whatever way they looked at it. Carlton would not have wanted that for Missy. I reckon they came away from the cult because Carlton did not go with these extreme thoughts of the cult."

"And yet he agreed with the whole female degradation thing in the house?" asked Hope, raising an eyebrow.

"Yes, but he did not see it as degrading, rather protective and allowing beautiful loved ones to show their full colours. I know it sounds weird, and yes it is. But that's where he's coming from. He sent Missy away so as not to taint the others. But now, as the family needs each other with the death of Liberty, she's back in the house. Yes, he struggles with Missy but he loves her."

"But what about the fuel and that? Surely he was involved."

"He realised what Ven had done. Ven had been brought up in the culture of that cult and he did what the cult law would have demanded. His father must have realised and then tried to spread the blame to the neighbour. But he was protecting his son and trying to protect the family as well."

Hope frowned in horror. "And when we took him away, we left the door open again for Ven."

"Yes! That's it exactly."

"So all that remains is to find Missy, put Ven under pressure and find her body. She's probably dead."

Macleod nodded. "I think so but we'll put him under pressure and find out. At least find a body for her mother to bury."

"One screwed-up family." Hope turned away and made herself a coffee. "You know, Carlton did have that look you men have, that disgusted one. You have it sometimes."

"How do you mean?"

"Well, I remember the first time you saw me in the station house in Glasgow, before we set off for Lewis. I'm not sure you were happy with what I was wearing. A bit flirtatious for you maybe?" Hope smiled but Macleod sensed the seriousness of the question.

"Yes, I could see your underwear."

"Underwear?"

"Yes, a bra strap and some cleavage. When I grew up, that would have placed you as a woman of some ill repute. But that's not how I see you."

"Thank God for that," said Hope.

"Indeed, thank God. But it is uncomfortable to me. Yet when Jane roams the house in just a sh—"

"What?" exclaimed Hope.

Macleod smiled at his runaway thoughts. "You see, different standards. We have different ideas of private, men and women alike. I'm sorry I gave you that look because you are something quite special, Hope."

"And you are an ever-revealing can of … beans?"

Raising an eyebrow, Macleod smiled. "However, you need a touch of eloquence, knock that city talk out of you." As he turned away he heard the words "Posh twat." Inside he laughed. Yeah that's me, arrogant, posh idiot.

# Chapter 22

Macleod believed this would be over fast. The man was only twenty-four, still a boy in Macleod's eyes, and he was banged to rights. The father, Justin Carlton, had caved in and admitted he was protecting his son. All they had to do was put on a little pressure and find Missy. She was probably dead, but he would continue at a pace until that was established for sure.

Macleod watched them bring Ven Carlton in through the rear door of the station and was once again impressed by the lad's stature. Someone of his strength would have had no problem subduing Andy MacTavish and Liberty Carlton, never mind Anna Campbell. He tried to remember the attacker in the bothy he had fought, but his memory, or maybe the original event, was not clear enough. He knew he'd been overpowered but he remembered so little of the attacker.

"You ready for this, sir?" asked Hope, approaching him.

"Yes, Hope. I just gave Jane a quick ring and she's back at our digs, got a bottle of red and sounds in the need of company."

"Shall I just move out to a hotel?"

"That would be ideal," Macleod said, his voice deadpan.

"Don't count your chickens yet," retorted Hope. "These things have a habit of continuing long after the detective thinks it's over."

Macleod stuck out his tongue before taking his coffee and indicating they should enter the interview room holding Ven Carlton.

The man was sitting down behind the rather sterile interview desk and seemed a little agitated. Good, thought Macleod, this should be easy if he's that worked up. Looking at Ven, Macleod decided he would let Hope start the interview and, after stating the important interview details on tape, he simply indicated to her that she could begin with an open hand.

"You know why you are here, Ven?" asked Hope.

"Its Vengeance, not Ven. Mother named me Vengeance. Said as a man I would be there to keep everyone in check. Liberty was kept in check."

"Did you keep her in check?" asked Hope.

Vengeance Carlton stared at her, his eyes seemingly cold. But then a tear fell from his left eye and ran down his cheek. Making no move to wipe it away, he shook his head.

"Did you like your sister? Was she well behaved in the house?"

Macleod saw the hands of the man now shifting uneasily. Although the interview room was warm, it in no way justified the sweat that was beginning to form on the brow of the man. Ven looked briefly at the floor before turning to one side and staring at the wall.

"Answer the question, please," said Hope. The man continued to stare.

"My colleague asked you to answer the question, Mr Carlton. Kindly do so."

The man immediately focused on Macleod. "Yes, sir. Dad seemed happy with her, I never saw him get angry with her.

Not like Missy, he didn't want Missy in the house. She had gone wrong."

"And she had to be punished? Like Liberty was punished? Is that what happened, someone had to punish them, sort out your sisters? Did the rules mean that?" asked Hope.

The man ignored her until Macleod prompted that the question needed to be answered. Then he focused once again on Macleod and the detective felt his partner's annoyance beginning to overflow as she snorted slightly.

"Liberty was with someone she should not have been with. She was in the wrong, with someone she should not have been with. That's why she was killed. The scroll was in her mouth. She's trapped now, not able to ascend, not in heaven. I won't see her again." Ven's eyes became very distant as if he was remembering something else.

"Was it right what happened to her? Did she deserve it?" asked Macleod, taking the lead due to Ven's repeated ignoring of Hope.

"They used to do that in America when we were there. That's what father said. They used to do that. But…" Ven fell into silence.

"But what, Mr Carlton?" The man remained silent and Macleod leaned forward over the desk. "I asked, 'But what?' Answer me, please."

"But there the fathers did it, was a father's right to do it. He should have done it. She should have been more like Mother; she's a good example of how a woman should be." The man turned his head now to Hope. "You would benefit from her example. Dressing like that is not for outsiders."

Macleod looked at Hope and while she was wearing an outfit that showed off her feminine curves, it was by no means vulgar, even to Macleod's higher standards of decency.

"Did the same thing happen to Missy that happened to Liberty?" asked Macleod.

"I don't know," said the man angrily. "They asked me that at the house and I told them I didn't know. I still don't know."

"When did you see her last?"

"It was this morning. At breakfast, before I was given chores to do with Sera. I was with Sera in the work room, clearing it out."

"The work room?" prompted Macleod.

"Yes, Mother's room where she sews and makes the clothes. She wanted it cleaned out, turned around and for Sera to help me. She said it would keep us going for an hour but it took longer, maybe three. Then we heard Missy was gone and they asked me a lot of questions. But I didn't know where she was. I still don't. You took Father and that meant I was responsible for Missy, but I don't know where she is. Have you any idea?"

The man now stood up and paced the room. "Father would have known where she was. He'd have found her, but you put him in here. You'll never find her. Father said you didn't find Liberty until it was too late. How are you going to find Missy? She should be with us. She should have stayed at home with us, should have let Father find her someone good to love her, one she could be at one with. She could have been as beautiful as Mother."

"Are you saying you haven't seen her or been with her since this morning?" asked Hope, interrupting. The man ignored her. Macleod went to speak, but Hope beat him to it. "I think you took her and have placed the same scroll in her mouth as you did for Liberty. I think you did it."

"Shut up," yelled Ven. "It's not your place to say it, not your right to accuse. I haven't seen her. It's not me, it's not me, but I failed, I failed." Vengeance Carlton now stood up and brought his fists down on the table, thumping them hard enough to make it shudder and move. "I have failed, like Father I have failed!"

With that, he grabbed his chair from behind him, throwing it off the wall. "Calm down," shouted Macleod, but the man continued to kick the table before upending it, sending coffee everywhere. Hope raced round the table as Macleod called for help from outside. Hope grabbed Ven's arm and tucked it behind him, dropping him to his knees, and managed to handcuff him after a short struggle.

Reinforcements had arrived by this time and Macleod requested the room be reset while Mr Carlton was placed in a cell. Standing at one side of the room, Macleod kicked the wall.

"Didn't go well, sir?" asked Ross, walking into the room.

"No Ross, it did not. Get up to the Carltons' and rip that place apart. We'll give Ven Carlton another go but something is telling me he won't talk. Find me something to go on because we need to find her, fast too if she's got a chance of survival."

"Sir," acknowledged Ross and left quickly to organise his colleagues.

"Sir?"

"What McGrath? What?"

"Do you still think he did it? He got pretty frustrated there."

"And whose fault was that?" Macleod said and tutted.

"You said to take the lead."

"Take the lead, but when I cut in because he wasn't speaking to you then what made you butt back in? He was talking and you made him mad. McGrath, you could have cost us with this one."

"But are you sure he did it?"

"Of course I'm sure. His father's protecting him, that's obvious, and the guy himself shows all the traits and prejudices to do it. He's been brought up to hate, to tow the line, and ultimately to sort things out. He's not the quickest specimen either but looks as strong as an ox."

"But we don't know yet," said Hope. "There's no definitive proof. He said he was with Sera today so how is he going to hide Missy away? Let me go up with Ross to the house. I want to do more digging up there. I'm not convinced."

Macleod shook his head. "Are you sure this isn't your ego being bashed because you sent him nuts? You're not put out because he wouldn't speak to a woman."

"Don't go there! I'm a detective, not some dizzy bird who gets all uppity because someone had a fit before them. No, sir, I need to follow this because I think we have this wrong."

Macleod turned his back. "Okay McGrath, go with Ross but make it quick because if you're right we're going to look like asses when more happens."

"More? Beyond Missy what would there be?"

Macleod now faced Hope and lowered his eyes. "Liberty betrayed the family, as did her lover. Missy betrayed her sister and family. Anna Campbell, outsider who merely brought Liberty into contact with the outside world. Where does it stop with this logic? If I'm right, we've stopped it here and now. But with your idea, who knows when it'll stop because we don't have the killer anymore and everyone who's been in contact with these girls is a target."

Hope nodded and left the room. Blast, thought Macleod, I'd better ring Jane and give her the bad news. He left the interview room, and the crew cleaning it, and proceeded outside to the rear of the station taking in some air. Taking his mobile in his hand, he brought up the contact listing for Jane and looked at her displayed image. It was in a moment of laughter and she looked great. With his thumb he tapped the image.

And then he tapped the cancel button. Walking across the car park, he stood in front of a bush that was bare, stripped of its flowers in the winter. The slush made a slap as his feet hit it and the cold managed to bite into his cheek. He looked up and saw a sky that held less than half the stars he expected. It was cloudy, heavy clouds too.

What do you think? Have I got this right or is Hope on it? I was so sure until she said that, so sure. Anyone else I would have chewed out and told to clear off. But she's like you, so very like you. Able to get in under my skin to get the point across.

I miss you, love, even though you never saw this. You would have loved the mystery of these cases, the details. You understood people too, more than I did then. You would have made a great detective. Her face was before him, the brunette hair and once bright eyes that had faded after their marriage and the accursed interference of the community around her. It's good to talk, better than when we were together. I wasn't good at talking back then. Maybe I'm not that good anymore either.

"Sir, we're ready whenever you are." It was a constable at the back door.

"Coming. Thank you." I must have looked strange to him, talking to you. Standing here in the cold, not even a cigarette in hand, or a vape, think that's what they call it. Probably looked tragic, a daft old sod talking to his dead wife.

But Macleod knew that wasn't what worried him. It was his desire not to talk to Jane about any of it.

# Chapter 23

Hope watched the road emerge from the darkness in front of her, a white covering having recently been dusted onto the surface. The road out to the Black Isle turned off the A9 onto a mixture of farmland and small villages, some with harbours and the obligatory pub. But they were heading to the far end of the isle and so she settled back until they were climbing out of the village of Rosemarkie. Whereas before there was a general darkness with lights punctuating it from nearby houses, they were now into a winding road with trees looming above, the trunks swept by the beaming blaze of the car lights.

"You from here, Ross?" asked Hope, watching the man drive.

"Yes, but from Inverness itself. I live out near the bridge."

"The big one?"

"Yes," replied Ross. "Why do you ask?"

"Have you ever heard of this cult over here before?"

"Never." He swung the car around another tight bend.

"Never heard of it in Glasgow either." Hope stared out of the window, trying to trace the dark shapes around them. "What's your take on this? Do you think Ven Carlton killed them all?"

"Well, looks like him or his father. Maybe his father the first two and then was daft enough to ask the son to help out with

Missy. Or maybe the son did it off his own bat. Who knows? But my money's on the father, despite what your inspector says."

"So this is a wild goose chase then, coming up here?"

"No," said the man, shaking his head violently. "She's gotta be up around here somewhere. Probably dead though."

"Tell you what, Ross, drop me at the neighbours' first. I want to ask Mr Tunnock a few questions."

"You don't think it's him?" asked Ross.

"No, but he might help. He's a nosey bugger."

Having been dropped off at the top of the driveway, Hope made her way down to the front door of the Tunnocks'. She rang the doorbell admiring the attractive door again and found Alison at home.

"Excuse me, Mrs Tunnock, but is your husband home?"

The woman eyed up Hope suspiciously. "Why? What's he done now?"

"Nothing as far as I am aware, I just need to ask him a few questions. Where's he been all day?"

"He was out on the farm early on and late afternoon but otherwise he's been in that room of his with the telescope."

"Good," said Hope firmly, "he may be of some use."

Mrs Tunnock led Hope along and through to Jim Tunnock who broke off looking through his telescope to say hello to Hope.

"It's always good to see the better half of the investigation duo. Would you like a drink?"

"Jim, she's working."

"Okay, Alison, no need to be so strict, I'm sure the detective can answer for herself."

Hope reckoned another marital war was on the cards and

took over the conversation. "No, Mr Tunnock, nice to be offered though, but I am on duty. Were you looking over at the Carltons' place today? There's no need to appear offended; in fact, you might be able to help."

"Oh," said Jim, "interesting. I was actually casting a glance that way, what with the old man getting taken away. More commotion going on now too."

"Yes, we are investigating a missing person," said Hope.

"The older one?"

"Jim, how do you know?"

"Alison dear, can I ask you to make the officer a cup of tea? I'm sure that's allowed on duty."

Hope was not in the mood for tea but she did want to corner Jim Tunnock while he was alone and so nodded her assent enthusiastically. Alison Tunnock half stomped her feet before disappearing off like a scolded wife.

"So you saw her today, did you?" asked Hope.

"No, but I was trying to," said Jim. "Bit of a looker like yourself, the older one. Still remember her in the bikini out back before she left. When she came back, I did watch for her. She often would go out the rear of the house to take the air as they say. Got some serious curves."

Hope moved closer to Jim and sat on a chair in front of him. She leaned forward aware that she would be displaying some cleavage and holding his attention. "What did you see? You can tell me, your wife's not here."

"Well, nothing today. Yesterday she was out in a T-shirt in this weather and she looked fabulous. Got a figure like yours, can fill a top. I can see you don't mind me saying."

Hope felt a little sick at the comment but she had him where she wanted him and so kept up the image. "Anyone else out and about?"

"Well, I saw the mother, that Sera and her brother out the back earlier. But they were back in the house soon after. But their mother was down the fields shortly after that. Actually that threw me because I was looking in the wrong direction. I had had eyes on the garden at the rear but she was coming up from the field. She was quite far down too. And then she was coming out of the house, which was weird. I must have been daydreaming."

"You said you saw her earlier too?"

"Yes, I was in the field then and she was coming down from the house. I whistled to her because she was in some tight leggings and that, but she turned and ran back to the house. Or at least in that direction."

"How was she?"

The man lifted his eyes and smiled. "Hot and flustered. You could see she'd been sweating and was in a hurry. Her top gripped like—"

"No, more about her state, not her figure."

Jim Tunnock looked down at Hope and seemed to drink up the view. "She was sweating in leggings and you need to know more."

In her mind, Hope vomited. This guy was a proper sleaze ball. But she sat there drawing the information from him. "Was she carrying anything?"

"No. Nothing. But she seemed in a hurry."

Hope smiled. "How strong would you say Mrs Carlton is?"

"She'd put up a fight like you. Be worth it though."

This was too far and Hope breathed a sigh of relief when the door opened and Mrs Tunnock entered with a cup of tea. Hope stood up and collected the cup from the woman before walking over to the telescope in the room.

"Careful, don't touch his play piece," warned Alison. After the first encounter Hope had had with this couple, she noticed the new lack of tension in the air. Previously they were at each other's throats, but now there seemed to be a different charge to the air.

"Forgive me for asking, Mrs Tunnock, but don't you get a little pissed off with your husband ogling women through this telescope?"

A smile came across the woman's face and she sidled up to her husband and placed an arm around him, snaking one of her legs around his. "It's how he found me, all those years ago. Couldn't keep his binoculars off me. My husband is a voyeur, Detective, he likes to look but he has good taste."

"Again forgive me, but your husband does more than look." Hope watched the woman to see if there was any tensing up at the jibe, but neither of them flinched.

"And I do more than look as well. I am not a put-upon wife, Detective. We are more open than most couples, it works for us both. You should bear that in mind, might be an option for you in life."

"You'd certainly have no end of offers," interjected Jim Tunnock.

Hope felt her skin crawl. She didn't mind men looking at her but he was positively gawping with another woman on his arm. She was no piece of meat. She wondered if the next-door neighbours had a more healthy view of marriage. But then again, there was no such thing as normal in this job.

Hope drank her tea pondering her next question while the now happy couple seemed to fawn over each other. You'd have struggled to remember that one of them had recently been with a murder victim and had been a suspect. Maybe the relief of no longer being under suspicion was doing them a favour. They did say the power of fear, or at least fear now gone, was an aphrodisiac.

"When we found the fuel in your garage, did you have any idea how it got there?"

"None," replied Jim Tunnock. "I don't open the garage often and I keep it locked. Possibly the longest time it's been open is when I take a stroll down to the end of the field. My wellies, you see. It's been getting mucky recently what with winter and snow."

"How long would it be unattended?" asked Hope.

"Maybe twenty minutes tops. There're some things in there not for public consumption, if you know what I mean. Nothing illegal, but very horny shall we say."

Hope's mind raced and then pulled up quickly. She really didn't want to know more. There was a window of opportunity there to plant the gear but you'd have to be nearby to be able to see. You'd have had to have watched previously, known that the door was only open for that brief period. It would not have been by chance.

Hope thought about who could see what from the neighbours' house. It was cold outside and she was not in the mood for a walk through the snow, especially with a man who would surely be gawping at her arse, but such was the life of a detective.

"Mr Tunnock, I wonder would you take me along the route of your garage and then down to the field where you would have gone during the twenty minutes the garage door was normally open for?"

The man gave a shiver. "It's bloody cold out there, not really minded to be honest."

Hope turned to him and drew herself up proud like a peacock before walking over to the window. She stretched her arms out, rolling her shoulders and making sure the couple got a good view of her.

"I think we should all go," said Alison and Hope heard the husband agree.

"It'll be fun," he said.

No it won't, thought Hope. The things I do for this job.

A few minutes later, Hope was being guided over to the garage of the house before being pointed to the field at the back. She was glad she had her practical boots on rather than any fancier shoe as the snow was thick and cold, her feet disappearing to the ankle at times. Despite asking to be shown the way, she found that her guides seemed to manage to place themselves behind her and she again thought of herself as cattle being paraded before the buyers.

As she trudged down the field, she kept looking back to see which windows of the neighbours' house could still be seen. There was only one and it had a light on at the moment. Hope kept it in view as they reached the bottom of the field.

"And this is it, Mr Tunnock, as far as you went?"

"Yes, Detective, but call me Jim."

"I'm on business, Mr Tunnock, so it will stay formal." This comment seemed to have the opposite effect to that intended and she watched herself being assessed again.

"Jim likes strong women, Detective."

"I didn't realise he had a preference; as far as I could tell, boobs, bum and legs were all that was required." Again the comment was received too well for Hope's liking. "Tell me, Mr Tunnock, was there anyone in that room when you were down here?" Hope pointed at the lit window.

"Not that I can recall but it was daylight, much more difficult to see to be honest."

With all she wanted to know acquired, Hope quickly led the retreat back to the house and welcome warmth. She thanked the Tunnocks for their help and was led to the door by Jim Tunnock.

"Delighted to be of help," he said, his eyes roaming Hope. "If I can be of any more assistance, professionally or—" he paused here "—unprofessionally, then please, I'm all ears."

Turning her back to the house, Hope gave a casual thank you and walked quickly up the white drive. She wrapped her arms round herself feeling cold. Or was it shivers generated from a different feeling? Either way she was happy to be moving on.

# Chapter 24

Macleod was not happy. McGrath had put a spanner in his train of thought and he could not shake it. It had seemed so obvious, that the father had taken on the cult's beliefs and dispatched his child. But then, when he was arrested and things were still happening, it must have been the son. Having interviewed Justin Carlton, Macleod was convinced he hadn't done it, which left the son. And after talking to the son he reckoned he had the man he wanted.

But Hope was not convinced. So who else could play their part in this and why? The motive was coming from the cult so if he thought about it logically, anyone signed into the cult's beliefs could have done it. So Mr Carlton or his son, no doubt brought up on a diet of his father's words. The girls of the family, the mother? She had seemed so distraught when they had been round after the murders, anxiously waiting for her daughter. She had been the go-between when Missy had come back to Inverness for a visit to see her sisters on the sly.

Stepping out from behind the desk he was hovering around, Macleod called over a young police constable and asked him to take Mr Carlton into interview room two. There was a curt nod of the head and Macleod watched two feet scamper away. I need to know this family better, he thought. Anyone outside is not making sense. Our station manager, the publicity expert, but she's no killer. MacTavish's wife was not up to the job, and why the second killing? She actually showed a care for MacTavish. And the scrolls were too much for anyone thinking of planting the idea. A lot of thought to make that detail, to simply find the detail.

No, the family is the key and the son is the perfect target for all the hatred passed down about women. But I'll get hold of Carlton and make sure.

Macleod walked purposefully to the interview room once the young constable called back, advising all was ready. Justin Carlton was still a nervous wreck.

"Have you found her? Is it bad news? Is she...?"

"Easy," said Macleod. "I need to talk to you about your family. Tell me about when you went to America to join this movement you belonged to."

The man stared wide-eyed at Macleod. "But have you found her? I need to know, I have a right to know."

Macleod did not want to tell the man much but he needed to calm him down. Beside Macleod was a constable who had been told to simply sit in but Macleod could see the eyes on him, eyes that were looking to learn. He felt he was on a pedestal and his problem with that was you only ever heard about people falling off them, never about managing to stay on.

"Nothing so far. But we are looking. I need your help, I need you to answer my questions so I can help Missy. Do you understand?"

Mr Carlton looked down at the ground, and when he raised his head next, Macleod saw a tear in his eye. "She's mine, you understand, my child. Whatever she's done, she's mine."

"I understand, so help me. Tell me about moving to America."

The man fidgeted and then looked up at Macleod. "We were young, well, she was anyway. I had nearly reached forty and she was just eighteen. When Precious told me she wanted to spend her life with me, we went to her parents and they hit the roof. She never liked her father, always told me he was weak. She wanted a strong man like me. I found that funny then, I was like any other man, I could hold my own but I wasn't anything beyond the norm. But she saw something else.

"Then she said she had heard of this place where we could be with strong men and proper families. I didn't really know much, but, to be honest, life wasn't great, my job as a joiner sucked and I had an eighteen-year-old beauty telling me she wanted to run off with me to a place where men ruled the roost. You can understand why I didn't hesitate much."

The man was talking fast but the detail was coming out. Macleod sat back in his chair and awaited the whole story, deciding to stay out of the way as much as possible. "Go on, Justin."

"Well, at first it was great. They had these compound rules, which meant the wives and that were walking around looking like something from a wet dream. But there was also strictness, no messing about with each other's wives or that. It was in a lot of ways safe. That's when she got a new name too. Precious used to be called Anne but they changed it to Precious. She loved it too. I didn't get why."

"And you never asked her?"

"I was a middle-aged man with a woman half my age who was happy to keep her man satisfied in every way. Of course I never asked, it was like paradise!"

"And the dress code, that came from the group?" asked

Macleod.

"Yes. But again Precious loved it, loved me watching her all day. I enjoyed it too, I am only human." The man paused as if reflecting.

"So what happened to break up paradise?"

"I don't know about this for sure, but there were rumours one of the daughters was killed by her father. She was unhappy in the compound, constantly broke the rules with regard to who she could see and meet, clothes too, wanted her own way of dressing. I didn't see a problem with the girl, but then she disappeared and they said her father did it. The police were called in and the group started talking about things like purification. You see there was a religious aspect to it all, not that I believed any of that nonsense. Precious liked it."

"Purification? Tell me more about it," asked Macleod.

"Well, it's like when a girl doesn't behave as a woman should then she no longer deserves to be here. Not serving her purpose you see. So she's dispatched. That's the word they were using too, dispatched. About their own daughters and wives." Justin Carlton shook his head, his eyes starting to stream. "The girl who died was only sixteen, had been seeing a local lad apparently. She was lovely, truly lovely. Feisty but kind, a free spirit but a good one. Do you know what I mean?"

Macleod nodded, watching the man begin to choke up. "Maybe I could have stopped it but I didn't speak up. Instead I decided we needed to get out. Precious wanted to stay but she was stuck. According to the group rules, she had to obey me. But she sulked. I told her we would go to Scotland, back home, and promised to set up our own little group. And I did. She was happy."

"So you lived within the group rules? Did anyone else join

you?"

"No," said Carlton. "I saw what had happened before, how extreme it had gotten. And I was happy. We had a family, Precious was teaching the kids about what she believed and I was happy with my family. I ruled my castle, we had a family." The man started to openly weep now.

"So what happened?" asked Macleod.

"Kids. I guess it's the same for every parent. They want to do their own thing. Missy was the start of it. She wasn't like her brother. You see Ven hung on his mother's words, they are very close. And it's done him good, he's very defensive of the family. The man's role you see, you not only rule the family but you defend them, protect them. That was the doctrine of the group.

"But Missy, she hated it all, the clothing, the being on parade as she called it. I guess she was right, but it rubbed up against her brother and mother. There were blazing rows and Precious told me I had to sort her out. In the end I sent her away. Hardest thing I ever did because she was mine."

Sniffing at first before breaking out into full tears, Carlton held his head in his hands. Macleod decided to wait for him and gathered his own thoughts. As the tears and sniffs grew less, Macleod leaned forward on the desk, hands together.

"When I spoke to Missy, she was angry at you for it. But I understand that Missy saw her siblings from time to time and her mother."

"Yes, yes, I instigated that. I couldn't see her myself, Precious wouldn't have had that. But the other girls were now going to outside school and making friends and I didn't want them to have the same struggles. So I encouraged Precious to make contact through Missy's sisters and to keep contact. Then she could keep an eye on them and help them if they were having difficulty."

"Did your wife take up that role gladly? It seems a strange one for her given her love of the group's rules and her beliefs."

"At first she refused, but I instructed her. And then she started to seem happy about it."

"So you were kept informed about Missy and the other girls' activities outside the family?"

"No, never!" The man seemed to doubt himself for a moment and then stared away. "Maybe if I had..."

"So who knew about the girl's activities? Your wife, the girls themselves? Ven?"

"Not Ven. He wouldn't have agreed with it."

"Would your wife have told him?"

"I doubt it. I would have been the one to be told. That was how it worked. Any rebuke was my action to take as head of the house. If I didn't know then I couldn't take action. America was always on my mind. I didn't want it all to..." The man broke down again.

"What? Didn't want what?" pressed Macleod.

"Didn't want it to go like America."

Macleod was on his feet now. "And when it did? Why didn't you tell us?"

"I protected my family. I'd lost Lib and I wasn't going to lose any more. I kept a close eye on them all, even let Missy back in. I had them all together, safe! But you took me in here." The man was now raging. "You bloody brought me in here. What could I do here? Tell me! And then you brought my boy in. He was looking after them."

With two hands on the desk, Macleod stood over Carlton. "But Anna Campbell died. My colleague was almost killed. I was attacked. How was that any protection? Someone tried to frame your neighbour. How was this protection?"

"You brought me in here! It was your fault!"

Macleod sat back down, a thought suddenly running through his head. "Ven … would he kill his sisters if they were out of line?"

"No! I never taught him about the scrolls and that religious shit! Not until after Liberty. I forbade Precious from telling him too. He didn't know about it."

"How strong is your wife?"

The man stared at Macleod. Suddenly his eyes seem terrified. "No! She wouldn't."

"She didn't want to leave America. She didn't feel anything was wrong about what was happening over there. She knew the girls' actions because you told her to keep an eye."

"But it was my right to rebuke them! It meant she couldn't."

"And when you wouldn't, when you created this impasse, this blockage to dealing with their actions, she took charge."

"But to kill our daughter, no!" The man stood up and beat the wall with his fists. The constable stood and went to approach the man, but Macleod held up a hand, stopping him.

"You said Ven would protect the family. Did she tell him? Did he try to frame your neighbour? Who did you think had done it? You knew, man, you bloody knew. And now your other daughter is going to pay. Anna Campbell died because you hid it all from us."

Carlton beat the wall again and then collapsed to the floor. "I hid it from myself. She can't have done it, she can't. She's their mother."

Macleod felt a shiver run down his spine. Yes, she's a mother but she's also something worse. She was and is a true believer.

Dear God.

He grabbed his mobile from his pocket. McGrath's with the killer.

# Chapter 25

Hope acknowledged the constable at the front door and entered the Carltons'. In the hallway she saw Mrs Carlton looking tearful. She was wearing a rather drab smock and her hair was crudely tied up behind her. As she recognised Hope's presence, Hope felt like she was being looked over, almost evaluated.

"Mrs Carlton, I was hoping to see Sera."

"Why do you want Sera?" The voice was bitter but then her husband and son were both being held at the station.

"Just some questions, nothing traumatic."

"I'll take you to her. She's in her room. Looking at photos of Missy, I believe." The older sister's name was spat out, like a piece of food waste stuck between her teeth.

McGrath ascended the stairs behind Mrs Carlton, aware of indignant shoulders before her. On reaching the appropriate room, Hope was invited to open the door and Mrs Carlton watched with hateful eyes as she entered. Hope gently closed the door and looked at Sera, lying on her bed, dressed in a similarly drab smock to her mother's.

"Sorry to bother you," said Hope.

"It's Missy, isn't it? Oh God, you've found Missy."

Hope held up her hands. "No, it's not. And we haven't. I

just need to ask you some questions." Making her way to the window, Hope pulled back the curtains and looked out on a nightscape that reflected the light of the moon off the crisp snow beneath. "Do you often stand here? I mean here at the window and look out. You can see lots, can't you?"

The girl looked somewhat anxious and sharply sniffed. "Why do you ask?" The shoulders were not steady and the voice wavered somewhat.

"Curious, that's all. Do you stand here often?"

"I don't like to but Mother makes me sometimes."

"Oh," said Hope, "why's that?"

"She gets worried about the man next door. He's always trying to look at us."

Hope felt a touch of guilt for asking the next question as she had felt Mr Tunnock's lingering eyes, but she needed some answers. "But he has a right to, doesn't he? He is a man after all, we dress for them."

The girl bowed her head before glancing at the door. Hope walked over to it and pulled it open. Looking up and down the landing she saw no one. "It's clear, she's not there. You can talk."

The girl raised her eyebrows and then followed Hope to the door. After examining the landing as well, she ushered Hope back inside and then stood at the window. "Come close so I can whisper." Hope stepped over to the woman and kept half an ear on the landing.

"Why do you have my brother?"

"He's suspected of being involved with the death of your sister."

The girl laughed, hollow and sarcastic. "Ven would not have killed Lib. He loved Lib, they were close friends, like Missy and me."

"But he is a man in this house, responsible for keeping you in line, dressed appropriately."

"Why do you say that? Ven is here to protect. Like my father, he only protects us. Protects us all. Whoever killed Lib," sniffed the woman, " it wasn't Ven."

"Then your father?"

"My father, what do you know of Papa? You have the two most gentle men I know locked up in a cell probably. They have done nothing except protect us."

"I don't believe you. They make you wear lingerie and other clothes that are not suited to a family setting."

Sera looked with incredulous eyes at Hope. "They want me to be beautiful, like Mama, like Lib was."

"Like Missy?"

"No," said the woman, standing up. "Missy flaunts her body, like you do. Do you know who that attracts? People like our neighbour. I want a good man, so Papa protects me until we find one."

"But it's your choice to dress and be how you want to be." Hope found herself becoming less dispassionate and starting to re-educate the woman. "You are in control of your body and how you appear to them."

"Am I? Are you? We are too much for most men, driving them to silly things."

"Liberty didn't think so."

"And she's dead!"

The room became silent and Hope made her way back to the window looking out. Her attempt to change the woman's thinking had run into the bastion that was engrained thought and to chip it away could take a lifetime. It would be better to get back to the task in hand.

"So Mama makes you stand here? It's very draughty. I mean really draughty."

"Yes, when she needs me to." The woman looked at her feet as she sat on her bed.

"Why?"

"To keep an eye. Sometimes Mama has to go down to the field beyond here. She likes to know if our neighbour is watching."

"So you watch over her the whole way."

"I try to but I rarely see her leaving the house. I pick her up further down. I give her a signal if he's watching."

"And does she do this often?"

"Yes, quite often. All us girls have used it, except Missy. She had left us when Mama found it. I don't like it. Lib used it, like Mama, but Papa should know."

Hope started. "Your father doesn't know about it?"

"No."

"How much did your mama know about Liberty's affair with the radio DJ?"

"She should have known nothing but I think she overheard things between Liberty and Missy. They spoke in a code, nothing complicated, and I think Mama knew all along what they were saying."

Hope came close to Sera, looking her in the eye. "She knew it all?"

"Maybe not all, but she suspected."

"Did she know about using the bothy?"

"They called it the hotel. But I think she knew it was something close."

There was a sound at the door, like the scuff of a foot on the wooden floor of the landing. Hope went directly to the door and opened it. There was no one there. She stepped out and looked around but again there was no one. She thought about looking in some of the rooms but that would prove nothing. Carefully, she closed the door and turned back to Sera.

"Do you know if your mama was in the house that day we found Liberty?"

"When?" asked Sera.

"The morning, in the morning, early. At daybreak or just before."

"She would have been in bed. I was in bed. Papa would know, he would tell you." The girl's face showed comprehension of what Hope was really asking, a deference to her mother's nature apparently. Hope wondered how the woman could not even ask the question of her mother.

Maybe she should ring Macleod and tell him of her suspicions, of how she reckoned the mother was the murderer. Yes, it seemed strange; after all, the woman had seemed so distraught that first time they had met. And where was she when Anna Campbell was killed, when Hope herself was attacked? Did she seriously get knocked out by this woman?

Hope took her mobile from her pocket and flicked the screen to open up her options. As she scrolled to Macleod's name, she heard something at the door. That foot scuffing, or whatever it was, sounded there again. Racing across the room, Hope flung the door open. No one was there. She entered the landing and saw a shoe disappear down the stairs. Following as fast as she could Hope took the stairs two at a time, but when she reached the hallway below, no one was there.

She opened the living room but it was empty. She entered the kitchen and saw a constable standing with a coffee in his hand.

"Did you see Mrs Carlton?"

"No ma'am. What's the matter? You came down the stairs like a herd of elephants."

Ignoring the comment, Hope raced around the house opening doors. She even checked under the stairs where a cupboard housed a hoover and some brushes. With nothing to be seen, she ran outside bumping into the female constable outside.

"Anyone come out? Mrs Carlton, have you seen Mrs Carlton?"

The woman shook her head. "No one's been out. Been quiet. Why?"

"She's gone, we need to find her. She's about somewhere. Find her—now!" Hope ran back inside where the other constable had put down his coffee and was beginning to look around for Mrs Carlton. Hope tore up the stairs and started opening doors. She first entered what must have been where Missy was staying, a room with a kit bag and no other clothing and devoid of any personal effects or photographs. Then she was in what had been Liberty's room. She remembered it being searched early on. There was a picture of the family, Missy blacked out with pen.

She's not going to be up here, thought Hope, she would have run. Surely she would have run. That means she might run to Missy, if she's still alive. Time's ticking, I need to find her.

Hope entered the bedroom of Mr and Mrs Carlton and saw a dressing table, which had a cardboard box sitting on it. It lay open and a marker pen was placed beside it. Some small pieces of notepaper lay scattered. Hope recognised it immediately. It was the same as the half-paper left over in Anna Campbell's mouth.

Her mind spinning, Hope tried to focus, to fixate on the problem and not the image of Missy burning that was beginning to flood her mind. She ran but she wasn't seen by anyone. She had to get out. But I checked everywhere and the two doors are the front and back. Front door was covered by the constable. The rear would mean she would have had to go through the kitchen. So where did she go? The passage, she's used the passage.

Hope raced back into Sera's room. The girl was sitting down on her bed, crying. At Hope's sudden arrival she looked up and Hope knew she had connected the line of thinking Hope had been on.

"No! No! She wouldn't."

"Where's the passage? How do I get into the passage?"

"The stairs," blurted Sera, "it's under the stairs. Move the hoover and the brushes, it's under the floor."

Hope did not wait for a response. Running down the stairs, she issued an instruction to the male constable to hold the back door and tell his colleague to cover the front door, just in case Precious Carlton was still hiding somewhere in the house. Opening up the door under the stairs, Hope threw out the hoover and then the brushes. She ran her fingers across the dark floor and found a small gap in the wooden surface, which enabled her to pick up a floorboard.

The gap was tight and Hope had to contort to squeeze her figure through the space. Although she was in trim shape, she was a stoutly built woman and the gap was thin. But she managed to make her way into the blackness below.

The surface under her feet was solid, possibly concrete or something of that ilk. The blackness was thick and she could not see in front of her nose. Running her hands across her jacket, she could not find a torch on her. She took out her mobile and activated the light app and soon had a dim view of the interior of the passage.

The sides of the passage looked like damp, cold concrete. Above her was also the concrete-like substance. The air was musty and thick but she could not smell any scent of a person. But then Precious Carlton wore no perfume. At least Hope had never smelt any on her. Carefully, she stepped forward, the small light giving just enough light to proceed safely up the corridor.

As she made her way along, Hope found the passage compressing, and soon it was barely a person wide and only some five foot high. She had to bend and her neck became sore as she held it at a tilted angle to see where she was going.

I must ring Macleod when I'm out of here, but if I'm quick I might pick up her track. I might see where she's going. I can ring once I'm out, let them know to follow. I need the light and I doubt I'll get a signal in here.

In her mind Hope was trying to gauge how long the passage would continue before it opened up into the little hut at the end of the field behind the Carlton house. Although the corridor was damp, she was sweating inside and she could feel her blouse sticking to her. Beads of perspiration ran down her face bringing a salty taste to her lips. She'd need a shower once she got clear of all this.

The light from the mobile showed the end of the passage and Hope looked up to find an open gap through which she could climb. She had to lever herself up with both arms and emerged into a small shed, the door of which was wide open. Outside she could see the piles of perfect snow, giving the night a cold glow, allowing the scenery to be dimly understood.

She held back from exiting the shed, listening intently. She could hear the wind outside, not so much whipping around the trees but moving them gently, though still causing a deathly swish to be heard. For another minute she stood completely still but the only thing she heard were the elements coming alive at night. There was the wind, the sound of the sea in the distance, and the fall of snow, which seemed to have begun since she had been in the house. Maybe it was her over-heightened senses but she could almost hear those flakes falling.

Hope took her mobile and killed the light app before placing a call to Macleod. Placing it to her ear, she heard the mobile try to connect, accept briefly and then fail. She placed the mobile before her and looked at the signal strength on the screen. One bar, flicking on and off. Maybe outside it would be stronger.

Stepping outside, Hope saw the reception bar come on for longer and quickly redialled. Again there was a connect but then a single tone indicating the line had dropped. She shivered, the falling snow making her cold as it landed on her hair and face, melting on contact. She would try the emergency line, it would grab any mobile provider and maybe she could get through. They'd soon get Macleod up here.

She rang three nines and waited for the answer. As it rang, Hope turned around and looked down at the ground near to her. She saw a footprint.

"Emergency, which service do you require?"

"Police," answered Hope without thinking, her eyes now scanning around her. The footprints seemed to walk around the shed and she followed them.

"Police. What's the emergency?"

"Detective Hope McGrath requesting assistance to—" Hell,

what do you call this place? "—my location immediately. In pursuit of a murder suspect. Contact Inverness station, Detective Inspector Macleod, tell him I am at the rear of the Carltons' house. There's a shed out the back, I'm at that shed in the field and suspect Precious Carlton has absconded."

Hope followed the footprints round the shed and found them coming back into the small building.

"Say again the address, ma'am."

Hope looked up into the shed.

"Carlton's place, Macleod will know it, anyone at the station will know it."

A spade suddenly filled her entire view.

"And confirm Detective McGrath requesting? … Confirm please, ma'am … ma'am confirm, please … ma'am?"

# Chapter 26

"Ross, get a car, we need to get up to the Carltons'. It's Precious Carlton, she did it all. I can't raise McGrath on the mobile. Get it up on airwave. Why are you waving your hands at me?"

Macleod had come running into the office as Ross had just put down the telephone. The whole time Macleod was speaking Ross had been trying to say something with his hands but to Macleod the man was making no sense.

"Emergency call from McGrath, sir, she's on the trail, Mrs Carlton's made a run or something. But the call was cut short."

"She tried ringing me. We need to get up there. Get some cars moving, Ross. And get a chopper, if she's running we need to see where. She might have Missy somewhere. Is anyone still up at the bothy site?"

"Negative," said Ross, "all done and cleared from there. Believe we pulled the last person from there this afternoon."

"Damn, we'll get some cars moving."

Macleod spun back out of the office and headed towards the cells. After motioning to the custody sergeant, he was taken to Justin Carlton's cell. The man was lying on the small bed-cum-bench and was crying.

"She's on the run, Carlton, your wife is on the run. She's

possibly got my DC as well. Where does she go? Is there anywhere she'd run to?"

"She won't run," said the man sitting up suddenly. "She won't run. She'll finish off her calling. They said it was the most important thing. To make an example, to teach the others. She'll do it for Sera, you understand me, she's doing this for Sera. That's why I left. I gave her something else so she wouldn't have to do this. I gave her a better version."

"Looks like cult-lite didn't work. Does there have to be a place? Is she going somewhere specific?"

The man was now doubled up and crying. He howled and Macleod tried to lift his head, to make some sense, but the man was gone, lost in a world of regret, remorse and terror at the woman he shared his life with.

Dear God, don't let me be too late. You hear me? Don't let me be too late.

Racing out of the holding area, Macleod saw Ross who indicated there was a car outside for him. Grabbing his coat and scarf from the office, he jumped into the car and was taken into the Inverness night by a tall police constable. As the car weaved out of the city and over the Kessock Bridge heading for the Black Isle, Macleod tried to ring Hope's mobile. But time and again it just rang out and went to voice mail. He rang Ross.

"Are we getting a trace on her mobile?"

"No point, sir, we just found it, a few seconds ago. It was at the shed in the field behind the house. There's a passage there, possibly from the house, we are checking it. Footprints in the snow but they are faint and are covering up. All we know is that they have started heading towards the sea."

"Towards the bothy?" asked Macleod.

"No," replied Ross, "opposite direction. Then they arrive at the beach and end at the line of rocks washed up by the shore."

"Can't they tell where then?"

"Negative."

"Anyone gone to the bothy?"

"Yes, have a car there at the moment, waiting for the report."

"Have we got a helo?"

"Negative. Snow storm moving in and they can't fly. Trigger lightening, the works."

"Can't they try to?" Macleod thumped the dashboard in front of him making the driver of the car jump. "I think she's going to murder whoever. Otherwise she would have stayed in the house. Setting an example; that's the most important thing. That's what Justin Carlton said."

"I'll try the helicopter again, sir. I'm sending everyone I can. I'll get the other agencies involved, see if we can get the coast searched too."

The car tore through the night, the roads being briefly lit up as they passed through Munlochy, Avoch and Rosemarkie. Macleod tried to gather his thoughts as they drove uphill from Rosemarkie, a road that swung here and there, the beam of the car highlighting the trees that heralded a large drop beyond.

In truth Macleod was oblivious to their position on the trip. His mind was engaged with possibilities he needed to check on arrival. Surely she'd go to the bothy. If Missy was alive, wouldn't she burn her at the bothy like her sister? But then Anna Campbell wasn't killed there. But she couldn't kill her there; they had still been at the bothy so she had brought her to another one.

When the car pulled into the snow-covered drive of the Carltons', there were already four vehicles there. Macleod strode from his and made for a constable at the front door. Despite the jacket and scarf, Macleod could feel the weather closing in and the snow was beginning to fall more thickly. Coupled with the wind that was picking up, he found himself having to shield his eyes somewhat.

"Constable, what's happening?" asked Macleod.

"The sergeant is at the end of the field, sir, with the rest of the searchers."

"How many do we have?"

"Five, sir, three of us here at the property."

Macleod nodded and made his way inside. From the hallway, he opened the living room door and found a constable with Sera who was in tears, sniffing away. Macleod was not in the mood for any games and didn't have much pity.

"Sera Carlton, where would she go? She's not at the bothy, so where is your mother? Where else did she go out there?"

"I don't know. With us the whole time, spying on us, that's what your colleague said. She said it was Mama that killed Lib. It can't be." The woman stood up in hysterics and grabbed Macleod's coat. She shook him violently, so much so that he grabbed her back, and with a grip normally reserved for miscreants he pushed her back into the chair she had risen from. Sera was clearly not going to be a lot of help.

Going back out to the hall, Macleod contacted Ross on his mobile. "Have you got any search teams yet?"

"Pulling them together, sir. We are stretched pretty thin across the area tonight. I'm trying to get a lifeboat to search the shoreline. With the way the weather's closing in as well it won't be easy getting a large turnout or even running searches."

Macleod wanted to yell at him, wanted to scream that his partner was missing and that he'd better get his foot up his backside and get people out here. But it was not Ross' fault. He was merely a man caught in the daily problem of manpower that all police forces suffered from these days. Government funding, for a multitude of reasons, was not what it had been twenty years ago.

"Keep at it, Ross," said Macleod encouragingly, despite feeling anything but. Macleod decided he would make his way down to the tracks they had found as they would soon disappear given how heavily the snow was falling. As he stepped outside the front door, he realised that he did not have his wellington boots with him and he gave a slight shiver at the thought of the shoes he had on. They were stout enough. Black and with a platform on them that accommodated one of the most comfortable insoles he had ever found, but they did not cover his ankle. He needed overtrousers too. Ross could get some sent up but there was little time, he needed to find Hope.

She had saved him before. From diving into the sea to fighting in a river, she had come to his and others' rescue. In the short time he had known her, Macleod had become fond of his partner. After fighting through feelings left behind by the death of his wife twenty years ago, Hope had brought about a resurgence in him, had helped bring him back to life. As much as she was coarse, dressed far too brazenly for his liking and, if he was honest, a somewhat sexual distraction, he had built up a respect for her. More than partners, they had started becoming friends. This heady mix meant Macleod was struggling to remain calm. Despite the cold, he was beginning to sweat.

He rounded the front of the house and made his way past the rear of the building and out into the field that led eventually towards the shore. Could Precious Carlton be heading for the shore? Was there a boat? Could she double back to the road from somewhere and pick up a car? Maybe he was overplaying this. She wanted to make an example not escape. She wanted to demonstrate. She had killed before in the place where the iniquity had happened. In the love nest, the shag pad as Hope would no doubt call it.

The snow was now deep enough to reach over his shoes and begin to wet the bottom of his trousers. He felt the top of his socks become cold and he tried to ignore his body shouting at him to get inside somewhere warm. Looking ahead, he fought to see and pulled a small pocket torch from his jacket. In the distance he saw some figures but could not keep his face peering into the storm for too long at a time. Grimly he trudged on along the field, past the shed where they had found the mobile.

He reached the end of the field and found two officers struggling to see into the night. They indicated that others had started off along the beach routing away from the direction of the bothy, pointing out the now almost vanished footprints they had found, a track they now followed.

"Can you get to a road if you go this way?" asked Macleod.

"Aye, sir," replied the officer with a deep voice that boomed into the storm. "It's a fair walk but you can. Maybe a half-hour walk though."

"Are there any jetties or piers nearby?"

"No sir, just beach round that way. Rocky outcrops here and there but mainly beach. We're waiting here to maintain a comms base as communications are difficult. Seems to be hard to get any signals here, even the airwave's not good."

Macleod nodded and stood looking along the beach, peering

along a darkened shore. Above the noise of the storm he heard the crash of the waves and was taken back to a cold Lewis sea and fighting for his life. He remembered Hope coming to the rescue, how she swam strongly in the sea, holding up the bag their victim had been in. The world owed Hope for that one, as did he.

"Constable, she's really on a hiding to nothing. And she's got McGrath in tow, presumably carrying her. Were the footsteps deep when you came down here?"

The constable shivered and wiped a drip off his nose. "Hard to be definite but yes, looked like someone could have been carrying someone else."

"Has anyone got to the road end from the other side?"

"They are on their way, sir. I doubt she'll get far going that way. There's only a single road out, we're cutting off the Black Isle as I understand it. I think we're in a good position."

"Very good, Constable. I'm going to cover off the other option in case she's been clever. I'll route along the beach towards the bothy and just make sure she hasn't double backed or anything. As you say, we're in good shape but best to cover all the bases."

The constable nodded, but before Macleod could turn away, he held up his hand. "Before you go, sir, no mobile signal all along that way. How long do you think you'll be so I know when to come and get you? Or do you want to take someone along with you? If you wait I'll get someone."

"Best get off," said Macleod, "so I'm back if anything else kicks off. I'll be as quick as I can, but if I'm over thirty minutes come get me."

Macleod watched the constable nod his head and then turn back to watch into the darkness on the other side. The heavy snow was now melting on his trousers, soaking them, and he started to feel the chill moving up from his socks. His hands were inside a pair of gloves but the cold was working its way through those as well.

He started along the loose rocks, slipping and sliding his way but trying to keep up a good pace. Every now and then he swung his torch around searching out into the swirling snow. All around looked like a winter scene but not one from a Christmas card. It was more like a horror, the eerie darkness challenging his mind as he saw shadows everywhere, which then dissipated in the ever-renewing canvas.

Macleod was not an edgy person but his nerves were being shredded as he was struggling to hear anything above the noise of the wind. His eyes fought to see through the falling snow and he felt exposed. His shoulders shook with cold as he rounded a small rocky outcrop and came upon a beach he had seen before. Set a little way back was a bothy, charred on the outside but now without the stench of death as the wind was blowing behind him.

He could not pick out any detail and he certainly could not say if anyone was there. Instead he routed to a large rock formation that had a hole cut into the middle of it. When at the bothy he had seen it but he had had better things to do. The sea swept in under the formation and had formed a man-high opening with its own small beach. Carefully, Macleod made his way round the outside. On the seaward side, he could see bare rock and scrabbled in the cold until he reached the opening. Dropping down, he found his foot submerged and quickly stepped ashore until he was under the rock. It broke the wind and Macleod looked around carefully. Again he swung this way and that with his torch until his eye caught something on the ground.

Walking over, he found a jacket, black like Hope's. Her warrant card was inside and he suddenly tensed. Turning now to the inside of the opening, he looked at the ground and saw footprints in the sand. Beside them was a long shallow imprint like something heavy had been dragged along.

# Chapter 27

Macleod reached for his mobile, struggling to use it with the gloves he had on. Frustration gave way to a mild panic as he then whipped off a glove and tried to ring Ross. There was nothing. He tried three nines, the emergency number, but again there was no signal. The cold bit into his gloveless hand as he stood and looked at the mobile. Blasted modern technology, a radio would have worked here, surely.

Donning his glove again and pocketing his mobile, he then knelt down to examine the tracks in the sand. Cautiously, he traced the track into the opening in the rock and made his way underneath the structure. In the dark he wanted to use his torch but he was unsure if anyone was about and he would rather not give up his position, shining a beacon for a would-be murderer. There were no shadows in the hollowed opening and he knew it was not just the cold that was making him shake.

Macleod tried to listen, but the swirling wind that drove the copious snowfall was blocking out almost everything except the repetitive crash of the waves coming ashore. Still, if it was covering up the sounds of an onlooker, it was also covering his own.

Deciding to work his way along the edges of the opening and abandon the tracks, Macleod gingerly fumbled his way to the rock face at the nearest side. His hands traced the crevices on the opening as he penetrated the darkness with a tepid foot. When the sudden shock of stepping into a puddle of cold water sent a shiver up his leg, he forced himself to stop swearing. This was crazy, he'd get his torch out and take the consequences. But then his hand found something plastic.

Tracing the outline, he realised that he was holding some form of container and his thoughts were confirmed when he shook it and heard the swish of liquid. The noise of the elements had calmed down somewhat now he was further inside the opening and sheltered to a degree from the wind. Fumbling around the container, he found a screw top and opened it. The pungent smell of petrol found his nose and his heart skipped a beat. She's going to do it again? Hope!

To make his way back would take time, time Hope, and maybe Missy, would not have. He would have to continue and then see what he could do. He hadn't found them yet anyway. Part of him thought about trying to light some fuel right there and then as a beacon for any further rescuers. But if he did, who was to say if that would accelerate Precious Carlton's plans, if they had not been accelerated already?

Leaving the fuel behind Macleod continued along the opening in the rock and managed to stumble his way through to the other side of the opening. Now the dim light, all but absent as it was, gave him some vague outlines to assess. In front of him was a large rock, several persons wide and at least a man tall. Up from it, he recognised the shape of the bothy. Macleod made his way to the edge of the large rock so that he could peer out at the building but keep himself hidden.

Being clear of the shelter of the opening, he was now subjected to the full force of the snowstorm again and the nip of the wind on his face cut in hard. His shoulders shook from the cold but he steeled himself so as not to stamp the ground or rub his body for warmth. Looking at the bothy, he saw no movement, but he knew Precious Carlton must be about. The marks in the sand gave away her actions, she must be there.

Macleod crept up slowly to the structure, which he remembered as having only a single entrance. There had been a small chimney, an outlet for any fire a camper would build, but otherwise only one entrance, albeit a fairly wide one, open the whole time. Maybe once there had been a door or covering, who knew. Reaching the side of the bothy, Macleod crept up to the opening and stood perfectly still. Someone was talking on the other side. With the wind assaulting his ears, he could not make out the words, but someone was in full voice, ranting away. Hopefully, he was not too late. This was surely a rant at someone who was alive. But he would need to see, need to enter via the only exit and make a confrontation with the hyped-up individual inside. Precious Carlton was not that strong, he could take her, that he knew. But then he recognised something in the air.

The bothy had been burnt out, and he had not been surprised coming close to it that he was picking up a charred tinge to the air. But there was something stronger now he was at the entrance. Something that set his nerves on edge. The smell of a garage forecourt, of spilt fuel, came to his nostrils. Had she already doused the building? Had she doused her captives? Herself?

Macleod flicked his head around the corner of the building

trying to sneak a look inside. The interior was dark, too dark to see anything. Cautiously, he slid around the corner and tiptoed inside the structure. The fresh scent of petrol was now overwhelming and he reached to his nose finding it damp with a drip formed. The howl of the wind was now outside and, although still strong, it was restricted to a background tapestry.

Macleod heard someone move up ahead and a liquid being poured. He thought about shining his torch but what would he do? If he set the beam loose, then Precious Carlton might have time to simply drop a match. He was guessing from the smell that the place was sodden with fuel. And that means my feet too, thought Macleod. But what should I do? Stumble about until I find her, a deadly form of blind man's bluff? Should I await help? But when will that come?

Maybe he could find Hope or Missy. He could drag them to the exit, give them a chance if the woman set the place on fire. That had to be the game here, get the captives free and not worry about an arrest. They'd catch up with her eventually.

He started to edge around the room. He could hear Precious Carlton muttering to herself even if he could not understand what she was saying. With his left foot he prodded to the side and, finding empty space, edged that way. Slowly, he continued along until his head hit something solid. It was an effort of will not to cry out. Thankfully, while the bump had been hard, it had not been loud.

This time Macleod went into a crouch, his arms out around him, prodding the darkness. His hand touched something and he soon realised it was a leg. He made his way up across the buttocks and then up the back. He nearly jumped but then realised his hand had been touched by the hair of the body that was lying prone. His hands continued and he found an ear and then the nose on the front of the face. The body gave a low murmur.

"Shut it! You keep quiet and take your punishment," shouted Precious Carlton. Macleod flicked his head to where the sound had come from. In the dark there was a small shaft of what passed for light coming in from a hole in the roof. It meant he could see a shadow and not much else. "Where's the blasted torch?"

Macleod raced away from the body as quietly as he could and was fortunate to be accompanied by an almighty moan from the prone figure.

"Shut it!" A torch shone onto the body and Macleod saw Hope's features, her red hair and her shapely figure. There was blood at the back of her neck, but she was breathing. In fact she was moaning, incoherently, but still moaning. "You're getting what's coming to you."

Macleod thought about trying to jump the woman but at the moment he had eyes on Hope and he needed to see if Missy was in the building. The source of the torchlight came closer and he saw a hand deal a slap to Hope's face. "Shut it. Chew on this instead, you hussy! Damn sluts in the police now, should know your place."

Macleod steeled himself not to react but the woman's tirade against Hope lit a fire in him. He had struggled with the rise of women in the workforce and, yes, he still thought this job was a man's job, like many other dangerous jobs. But he had adapted, he had worked with it and he had never accused the women who stepped up to these roles of being anything other than unwise. But this was horrible, one woman berating another for not being subservient to a man.

But as much as his mind reeled at this injustice, the smell of the fuel reminded him of his immediate problem and he thought he might be able to reach across and grab Precious Carlton. And then he heard the strike of a match. His heart jumped as he saw the yellow light take hold.

"Just one drop of a match and you will end, your flaunting will cease, jiggling your wares before my husband. And as for you," said Precious, turning around and shining the torch on a large piece of rolled carpet that was taped at the ends, "you will pay. You're no child of mine, no child of mine would be a whore, running around places like this, opening your legs to any man. You brought this family down, you corrupted Liberty, condemned her to a hell in the time to come. So you will burn and be with her."

Macleod watched the match keenly, deciding if he could reach it before it fell. As quick as it lit, however, it went out. He braced to move but another match was lit. Leaning back on his haunches, he knew he would have to make a move soon before this mad woman went through with her scheme. But if the fire started, he would have to chose who to save first. And there may not be a second chance.

The torch spun back around and he saw it light up Hope's face. Precious was now up close to her, a lighted match in her other hand, she knelt before Hope. The match was drawn back and forth in front of Hope's face and Precious taunted her.

"Look into the light, see how the fire will purify the place but not you. The scroll will keep you in hell, away from us, stop your taint from affecting us. If my husband was half a man he would do this to you. He would have slapped your face the first time he saw you rather than focus on your chest. Hussy! Slut!"

Macleod saw the rage rising and reckoned it could not be long until it spilled over and a match was dropped to set the place alight. Carefully, he sneaked up behind the torch. The brightness of the beam made seeing the shadow in front difficult and he threw himself forward trying to secure Precious Carlton's arm. One hand grabbed her arm, and before she could react Macleod had brought her hand and his other free hand together, his bare grip stifling the flame.

But he didn't clock her free arm with the torch. Precious swung her free arm at Macleod, the elbow connecting with his cheek and sending him spinning backwards to the floor. He tried to get up quickly, but in the dark his foot slipped and he fell over again. As he gathered himself, he watched in horror as another match was lit.

"You'll find them in hell," shouted Precious at Macleod, "along with yourself."

She took the match and dropped it in the box of matches she drew from her pocket. As Macleod stood up, she dropped the flaming box and ran for the door. And then flames erupted across the floor.

# Chapter 28

Macleod tried to scrabble to his feet as the flames spread. Precious Carlton had run out of the building and as Macleod rose he had nothing to impede his path to Hope except the flames rapidly spreading across the floor. Reaching down, he grabbed her under the armpits and began to drag her towards the door. She was heavier than he would have liked, and, in truth, it was more that he was not that strong rather than she was heavier than a woman of her shape would normally have been.

The flames leapt from the floor onto Hope's feet but Macleod did not try to stop their advance but rather made a run for the opening in the bothy. He saw the flames start to burn Hope's legs as he dragged her outside into the swirling wind of the snowstorm. He threw her into the snow, rolling her along, desperate to put out the fire that burned on her clothing.

The building then became ablaze, flames licking out the door and out of the chimney. Macleod took a look at Hope and believed she was okay, clear of flames anyway. Wrapping his coat around him as best he could, he looked at the flames licking the building and swallowed hard. Inside he was terrified, and it almost froze him to the spot. But he was a policeman, he had a duty, and the girl was unable to help herself.

He remembered Hope diving into the water off the Isle of Lewis, how she had fought so hard to keep their victim afloat, how she had saved the girl's life. Looking at Hope's face, her eyes rolling and unsure if she was even understanding him, he said, "Remind me to have the conversation with Jane. If not, tell her ... well, just tell her."

Macleod stood and experienced one of the strangest feelings of his life. His face was bitten by the cold and driving snow while also being burnt by the fire from the bothy. At the moment the cold was preferable. He raised his arm before him and ran in.

A surge from the fire drove him backwards forcing him to cower for a moment, his hands covering his face. Where there had been darkness there was light in abundance but a red and orange light that seemed to want to consume everything rather than illuminate it. In the far corner of the room he saw the rolled carpet. It was alight. He couldn't pick it up like that. Not with bare hands. Reaching inside his coat pockets, he put on his gloves again.

He stood up and tried to traverse the room. His feet were now on fire, the fuel he had stepped in had ignited his shoes and no stamping was putting them out. He sweated hard inside his jacket and his feet started to scream at him as they began to burn. There was no time. He ran forward, blundering on despite the flames that were thrown at him. In a few seconds he had crossed the room but his jacket was now burning and he was sure his time was up. But never had he given up without a fight. Even when his wife had committed suicide he had continued to go on. Somehow he had continued. And he would this time.

Macleod slipped his hands under the bag and felt the weight. He had to keep his head back to prevent the flames simply burning him but his arms became red hot incredibly quickly. Standing with his load, he staggered with the weight before girding himself and trying to run. The motion was awkward, his steps erratic, and when he tumbled to bounce off the wall it was no shock. His head took a crack but he staggered on. Within seconds, he emerged from the burning shell and felt the blessed snow rip into his face. But he was ablaze along with his load. He had only one thought and immediately began careering towards the sea. It was no straight line that he wove, rather a higgledy-piggledy curve that only roughly went where he wanted.

He heard the crash of the waves fighting above the wind to make themselves heard. There was a roar from the bothy behind him as the flames licked higher. All was pain for Macleod, but he was now running on pure survival instinct rather than reasonable thought. He felt the waves crash into him and he strode on, fighting with every ounce of strength he had. When he felt the water caress his waist, he tumbled forward dropping the carpet into the water in front of him.

With crossed arms he leapt on the carpet, looking to drive it down below the surface. Starve the fire of oxygen, starve it. He felt the cold of the sea on his face and welcomed it. With all his strength he looked to drive on down, further under the water. He would save her. Missy Carlton would not fall victim to her lunatic mother.

He surfaced and grabbed a breath before driving the carpet under the water again. His feet still felt on fire while his upper body was starting to feel cold again. Once again he surfaced and checked the carpet, looking for any flames. Either the fuel was done or the sea had dispersed it enough for the fire not to be burning on the surface. He needed to get the carpet ashore, needed to open it. His gloves were damp but they also felt like they were sticking to his skin. With one hand he grabbed the carpet and pulled it along in the surf until it touched the sand. Here it needed both of his hands to pull it and the going was slow. As he reached where the sea was at its furthest extent on the shore, he dropped down and tried to pull away the tape at both ends.

It was still hot and it took him two attempts to remove the tape and then unroll the carpet. The person inside was a mess but they were still breathing. Parts of the carpet had stuck to them and Macleod struggled to locate the mouth. As he bent down to check for life, something hit him on the back of the head.

He pitched to one side and heard a laugh. "Get off her, she's off to hell, you don't want to be with that hussy!" The venom in the voice caused a panic in Macleod and he rolled away as best he could on the ground, but his hair was grabbed and a blow rained down on his face striking the nose.

"Seoras! Seoras!"

It was McGrath's voice, but Macleod could not see her from his prone position. "McGrath, over here!" he shouted and received a kick in his back for his trouble. He rolled away again and then tried to stand up but found himself being pelted with rocks, maybe half the size of an adult hand. Turning his back, he saw a searchlight out in the sea. Reaching into his pocket, he found his torch and began to flash back, three dots, three dashes, three dots. He only made three dots before he was jumped upon.

Precious Carlton came down on top of Macleod as he

tumbled to the sand and his ear was bitten into. Desperately, he swung an arm, but he could not shake her off. He yelled as he felt the flesh of his ear rip. And then came a dull thud as if someone had been kicked in the stomach. The weight was released off him and his ear no longer felt like it was being torn, although it was still smarting in pain.

He was turned over and the wet, red hair of a familiar face straggled round his eyes. From the corner of his vision, he saw a figure depart in the dark, unsteady but most definitely escaping.

"Seoras! Are you okay?"

"Yes, but Missy, go to Missy." He watched Hope's eyes run over his face until she was satisfied and then she climbed off him. Struggling up to his knees, he saw Precious, a dim figure in the driving snow, starting to climb up the side of the rock structure with the hollowed-out inlet. The blazing fire from the bothy sent dancing shadows across the side of the rock face, but Precious was climbing the opposite side to the building.

Turning to the sea, Macleod saw the light again. It had increased in size and there was another smaller light. Someone was coming; Hope was dealing with Missy. "I'm going for Precious," he shouted to McGrath but did not know if she heard him. Hope was bent over Missy in what seemed to be mouth to mouth. Stumbling in the blizzard, he made for the bottom of the rock face.

The surface was reasonably smooth and Macleod, through eyes half closed due to the wind, scanned for the better footholds as he started his climb. It was by no means a sheer face and any child of ten would have bounded up the side in no time. But ten was a long time ago, and given the wind, snow and what he'd just been through Macleod was one of the slowest climbers this fixture had seen.

With an occasional glance, he saw his prey as she neared the top of the strange formation and he wondered where she could go. His hands stung, the half-burnt gloves sticking to them, and he was now in pain every time his hands grabbed hold of something. But she would not get away.

As he kept climbing he saw her come to a halt. She was standing against the wind, lit up by the orange hue from the fire. Her hair was loose and blowing behind her as the snow started to grab her clothes and accumulate in the thinnest amount on her side. Pulling himself up, Macleod stood less than six feet away. Only then did he realise how narrow the structure was at the top, a small pinnacle that had a drop to every side. The height was maybe forty feet but still a height not to fall from.

"She should be in there! She has no right to live!"

Precious Carlton was screaming at Macleod. Normally he might have made a move to contain such a person, but he was feeling unsteady on his feet anyway and there was the small matter of the drop below. Glancing around him, he saw a small boat beaching near to Hope.

"It's over, Precious, nowhere to go." As the words left his mouth, Macleod knew he was lying. There was always down, onto the rock and beach. But it would be a one-way trip.

"It doesn't matter, she's going to rot but I won't. I'll be there with Justin, though God knows I had to drag him there. So go back to your hussy of a partner. Go back, Detective, you can't touch me."

"You'll stand for murder. You killed your children, how do you do that? They grew up with you."

Precious turned and pointed down at the sand where Hope

was being joined by lifeboat crew. Macleod could see that CPR was still being attempted. Hope was shivering as she worked, the snow storm showing no abating.

"She corrupted them, she and her dirty swine of a DJ. Fornicating in that cess pit. Under my nose, they did it under my nose. I tried to keep them spotless, tried to show them how to be a good woman. But no, I was rejected. And she rejected paradise."

Inside Macleod was railing against the religious overtones. Having seen his wife's slow destruction at the hands of overzealous religious types, he fought hard to bring the professional policeman to the fore.

"You shall stand trial. You are under arrest, Mrs Carlton."

"What can you do? She's dead, dead and clear to live life in hell. You can't reach her now, Detective. No one can."

Macleod edged closer, desperate to take hold of the woman. He knew she was looking to simply end it, that she would jump when her moment in the sun was complete. Moment in the sun, way to pick the wrong expression, Macleod, it's Baltic. If he could only get close enough, take her down with a tackle; then she would face justice.

"No you don't," she shouted. "I see you, I know what you want. You won't take my prize, I have dealt with the sickness, I have cured the cancer. My family will join me soon enough. Goodbye Detective, swim in your own filth."

As soon as the word goodbye was uttered, Macleod dived at the feet of Precious Carlton. As she tried to jump, he landed beside her and threw his arms around her in a rugby tackle he would have been proud of twenty years ago, never mind now. His arms wrapped around one leg and Precious dropped to the ground cracking her head off the rock. As he smiled to himself, content he had his killer, Macleod felt his body begin to slide down the rock face ever so slowly.

"Seoras! Hold on! You stupid bugger, hold on."

As he continued to slip slowly along, Macleod saw Hope bound up the rock side. His eyes widened as she continued upwards, but he felt she would be too late. His descent continued and he realised Precious, now unconscious, was also slipping. The speed built up and he knew he was going down off the rock.

"Let her go, let her bloody go. Drop the cow!" screamed Hope. The wind swirled on and Macleod felt his sleeves move up on his jacket and a new cold hit his forearms. But he wouldn't let go. She would pay, she would be held to account.

And then it dawned on him, she wouldn't. And neither would he. The pace of his descent suddenly quickened and Precious slid off the rock edge below him as he was turned around and was left clinging to Precious as she dangled beneath him. He started to slide quickly and closed his eyes. This was it.

A hand grabbed his ankle and Macleod felt his left leg being pulled hard as if it would pop from its socket. He cried out in pain, but his descent had been stopped for the moment.

"I've got you, but I can't hold you both. Anyone, help!" Hope's words flew into the wind and Macleod wondered if anyone below could hear her properly such was the strength of the blizzard. Hope's nails bit into his ankle and he swore she had gripped deep like a butcher's hook. But his arms were struggling and Precious' legs were moving, slipping bit by bit from his grasp.

"Let her go! I'm starting to slip, Seoras. I said let her go."

His body slid forward and his torso slipped off the rock.

Beneath him, Precious was held by her ankles only, Macleod's arms wrapped tight. Above him, Hope screamed as she held him, one hand on an ankle. She must have been taking nearly all the weight.

"My hand's slipping. Seoras!"

"She needs to stand trial," he shouted. "She killed them, she killed her kids."

"And she'll kill you. Let her fucking go!"

He didn't know if it was instinct. Was it Hope's voice, the deadly earnestness in it? But his arms opened slightly. And Precious Carlton fell down, crashing off the rock before thudding into the sand. As he hung, Macleod saw the lifeboat crewmen run to her. And then he was sliding down slowly. He put his arms out to help push back. Soon he felt his jacket being dragged back and he was manoeuvred onto a ledge. Standing up, he felt a pair of arms wrapping him up tight.

"Don't do that to me, you bastard. You're worth ten of her. You're special, you hear?"

Macleod stood motionless, letting Hope hold him like the world itself was ending. "That's you bastard, sir!" And he grabbed her in return, holding tight, shaking on her shoulder.

# Chapter 29

The small, three-car ferry made its way across the firth from Cromarty to Nigg on a day that was cold but clear. The sun was shining but was rather low in the sky and Macleod wondered if the choice to sit outside at the low wooden crate tables was a good one. His fleece top was an expensive one, warmer than any he had been given before, but he was still feeling the cold through his legs. However, the coffee from this quaint house by the ferry slipway was very good and chased away any regrets about the weather from ruining his day.

The fleece had come courtesy of Jane. Macleod found it hard to believe she had stayed on here in Cromarty when he decided he needed some rest and recuperation. It was not her initial decision on hearing he was coming out from hospital but needed some weeks of recovery. She had, in fact, returned to Glasgow saying she had to get back to work and he had not expected anything else. Hope had a slightly longer stay in hospital but her burns had been worse than his.

He visited her daily in hospital in Inverness, getting a bus simply because it gave him time to sit and ponder the view. The Highland scenery was always breathtaking, especially as his mind was not on dark matters. His particular favourite had been seeing the water beyond the Caledonian stadium and its enormous expanse flanked by two green arms in the Moray firth. The Clyde in Glasgow had its own beauty as well as a real industrial heritage, but this was the wild on your doorstep.

Hope had stayed in the rented accommodation in Cromarty for a week after she had been released and they had taken some walks together, making it a daily ritual to climb the hundred steps. It was strange being around her without work forcing them to think beyond themselves. He had learned she was a lover of film and had even watched some raunchy art house picture with her. By the end of it, Macleod realised that there were things going on in American diners that he was unaware of but that health and safety should look into. No one should be cooking at a deep fryer wearing so little.

Hope had lingering burns, some that were likely never to leave her. She had shown him as they compared war wounds and his heart had been lifted, but then he realised that, as much as he enjoyed her company, there was a level beyond which they would not go. Not that in his mind during idle moments the scene of an intimate moment with Hope was not tested, but common sense was always there to prevent any real-life execution.

She had returned to Glasgow with business to attend to. Hope had not said what the business was, but Macleod was sad to see her go. During the week, he had barely spoken to Jane, but with Hope's departure he realised he had done something terribly wrong.

Missy Carlton had died. Despite the best efforts of Hope and the lifeboat crew, her burns had been too much. Meanwhile, her mother would make a full recovery or at least something close to it. Jane had tried to ask about how Macleod was feeling, but he had shut her down almost instantly. These were things for people in the job, and with Hope he had exercised the demons that had come with this case. And when he spoke to Jane, she knew he had jumped a hurdle.

Macleod finished his coffee but he felt hollow. It wasn't the beverage that was the issue but instead the fact that Jane had seemed to ring less. Or was it? She had been ringing every night but the conversations had been short. He had asked how Jane was, what she'd been doing, but her answers were short and then she'd ask about him. And the conversation wound up in five minutes.

He strolled along the Cromarty links and then stood on the beach watching the sandbank being covered over by the oncoming tide. He wasn't happy, he had failed the young woman; Missy was dead in every sense except his mind. Demons exercised with Hope, he thought. Bull!

He saw his wife's face and went to speak to her. But a pair of hands touched his shoulders and he nearly jumped before turning around. Jane's questioning smile welcomed him.

"Thought I should come and see you."

"You didn't need to," said Macleod, "I'm healing well."

"Are you? Are we?" Jane stepped up beside him and stared out at the sea. "I know you can't – or won't – talk about your work, and I get that, but you can talk about you. This wall, this silence when it comes to something that's bugging you, that's affecting you. I need in, Seoras. I don't want a fun fling. I love all that, but I want more. I want to know where your mind drifts off to."

Macleod looked at a seagull wandering along the rapidly submerging sandbank and realised that soon it would have to fly. Or swim. One thing was for sure, it couldn't remain where it was.

"Sorry, I haven't been fair."

"You haven't been here," said Jane.

"I've been talking to someone else. Someone close."

Jane swallowed hard and Macleod reached a hand over to her shoulder. "It's okay, at least I hope it will be. She's not competition, she's just someone who cared, who lit me up."

"And I don't? Am I just a fun woman to be about?

"You are a fun woman to be about. A figure that excites and challenges me, one I think who cares for me. She did too."

"Did?"

"Yes. She lives out there, in the water. Or in my head, my heart, my essence, call it what you will. But she doesn't answer." Jane looked at him quizzically. "Jane, you need to meet Hope Macleod, my wife."

The afternoon passed in deep and heavy conversation. Macleod wasn't sure how it went. But she stayed.

The End.

Turn over to discover the new Patrick Smythe series!

*Start your Patrick Smythe journey here!*

Patrick Smythe is a former Northern Irish policeman who after suffering an amputation after a bomb blast, takes to the sea between the west coast of Scotland and his homeland to ply his trade as a private investigator. Join Paddy as he tries to work to his own ethics while knowing how to bend the rules he once enforced. Working from his beloved motorboat 'Craigantlet', Paddy decides to rescue a drug mule in this short story from the pen of G R Jordan.

Join G R Jordan's monthly newsletter about forthcoming releases and special writings for his tribe of avid readers and then receive your free Patrick Smythe short story.

Go to https://bit.ly/PatrickSmythe for your Patrick Smythe journey to start!

# About the Author

GR Jordan is a self-published author who finally decided at forty that in order to have an enjoyable lifestyle, his creative beast within would have to be unleashed. His books mirror that conflict in life where acts of decency contend with self-promotion, goodness stares in horror at evil and kindness blind-side us when we at our worst. Corrupting our world with his parade of wondrous and horrific characters, he highlights everyday tensions with fresh eyes whilst taking his methodical, intelligent mainstays on a roller-coaster ride of dilemmas, all the while suffering the banter of their provocative sidekicks.

A graduate of Loughborough University where he masqueraded as a chemical engineer but ultimately played American football, Gary had worked at changing the shape of cereal flakes and pulled a pallet truck for a living. Watching vegetables freeze at -40'C was another career highlight and he was also one of the Scottish Highlands "blind" air traffic controllers.

These days he has graduated to answering a telephone to people in trouble before telephoning other people to sort it out.

Having flirted with most places in the UK, he is now based in the Isle of Lewis in Scotland where his free time is spent between raising a young family with his wife, writing, figuring out how to work a loom and caring for a small flock of chickens. Luckily his writing is influenced by his varied work and life experience as the chickens have not been the poetical inspiration he had hoped for!

**You can connect with me on:**

https://grjordan.com

https://twitter.com/carpetless

https://facebook.com/carpetlessleprechaun

**Subscribe to my newsletter:**

https://bit.ly/PatrickSmythe

# Also by G R Jordan

G R Jordan writes across multiple genres including dark and action adventure fantasy, feel good fantasy, mystery thriller and horror fantasy. Below are a selection of his work grouped together in their genres. Whilst all books are available across online stores, signed copies are available at his personal shop.

**The Horror Weekend (Highlands & Islands Detective Book 3)**
https://grjordan.com/product/the-horror-weekend

*A last-minute replacement on a role-playing weekend. One fatal accident after another. Can Macleod overcome the snowstorm from hell to stop a killer before the guest list becomes obsolete?*

Detectives Macleod and McGrath join a bizarre cast of characters at a remote country estate on the Isle of Harris where fantasy and horror are the order of the day. But when regular accidents happen, Macleod sees a killer at work and needs to uncover what links the dead. Hampered by a snowstorm that has closed off the outside world, he must rely on Hope McGrath before they become one of the victims.
It's all a game..., but for whom?

**Water's Edge (Highlands & Islands Detective Book 1)**

https://grjordan.com/product/waters-edge

**A body discovered by the rocks. A broken detective returns to a scene of past tragedy. Will the pain of the past prevent him from seeing the present?**

Detective Inspector Macleod returns to his island home twenty years after the painful loss of his wife. With a disposition forged in strong religious conservatism, he must bond with his new partner, the free spirited and upcoming female star of the force, to seek the killer of a young woman and shine a light on the evil beneath the surface. To do so, he must once again stand in the place where he lost everything. Only at the water's edge, will everything be made new.

The rising tide brings all things to the surface.

**Surface Tensions (Island Adventures Book 1)**

https://grjordan.com/product/surface-tensions

*Mermaids sighted near a Scottish island. A town exploding in anger and distrust. And Donald's got to get the sexiest fish in town, back in the water.*

"Surface Tensions" is the first story in a series of Island adventures from the pen of G R Jordan. If you love comic moments, cosy adventures and light fantasy action, then you'll love these tales with a twist. Get the book that amazon readers said, "perfectly captures life in the Scottish Hebrides" and that explores "human nature at its best and worst".

Something's stirring the water!

**Austerley & Kirgordon Adventures Box Set: Books 1-3 and Origin stories 1-3 (Austerley& Kirkgordon)**
https://grjordan.com/product/ak-box-set

*A retired bodyguard looking for a little fun before it's too late. An obsessive Professor, seeking the darkest things of life. And an Elder god seeking to rule the world, if they can't stop him.*

Join Austerley and Kirkgordon on the rollercoaster ride that is their first three adventures. Comprising 3 full novels as well as three accompanying origin novelettes, this collection will introduce you to a polarised duo that are the world's best hope. Joining them for the adventure are a myriad of strange characters, bizarre animals, evil humans and the UK's finest agents from its most secret department. As one reviewer put it, "If you like Lovecraft, Poe, or Conan Doyle you will like this book. If you like tv show like Buffy the Vampire Slayer, Supernatural, Being Human, or X-Files you will like this book."

So take a chance on a molotov cocktail of a duo and see how to save the world on the wild side.

**Scarlett O'Meara: Beastmaster: The Supernatural and Elder Threat Assessment Agency Book 1 (SETAA)**
https://grjordan.com/product/scarlett-omeara-beastmaster
*Cursed with a talent she never knew. Bestowed a gift everyone wants. Scarlett must embrace her mother's legacy to stop a lecherous shadow preparing a demon's army.*

"Scarlett O'Meara" is the first story in the urban fantasy maelstrom that is the SETAA series from the pen of G R Jordan. Featuring Calandra, the Ice Maiden from the well loved Austerley & Kirkgordon series, this tale introduces a buxom, feisty lass from the Welsh valleys to the strange powers that threaten to destroy our world. If you love plucky heroines, fantastic creatures and wild supernatural action, then you'll love these tales from Britain's most secret agency.

A relic bestowed great power on Scarlett. A demon removed that gift. Can she summon the true fire inside and save the world?Only with her back to the wall, will this girl shine!

Lightning Source UK Ltd.
Milton Keynes UK
UKHW040952040822
406842UK00001B/206

9 781912 153725